HOAXES
AND OTHER
STORIES

HOAXES
AND OTHER
STORIES

BRIAN DINUZZO

THE UNIVERSITY OF WISCONSIN PRESS

The University of Wisconsin Press
728 State Street, Suite 443
Madison, Wisconsin 53706
uwpress.wisc.edu

Gray's Inn House, 127 Clerkenwell Road
London ECIR 5DB, United Kingdom
eurospanbookstore.com

Printed in the United States of America
This book may be available in a digital edition.

Library of Congress Cataloging-in-Publication Data
Names: DiNuzzo, Brian, author.
Title: Hoaxes and other stories / Brian DiNuzzo.
Description: Madison, Wisconsin : The University of Wisconsin Press, [2022]
Identifiers: LCCN 2021038759 | ISBN 9780299334741 (paperback)
Subjects: LCGFT: Fiction. | Short stories.
Classification: LCC PS3604.I53 H63 2022 | DDC 813/.6—dc23
LC record available at https://lccn.loc.gov/2021038759

This is a work of fiction. Names, characters, places, and incidents are either
the product of the author's imagination or are used fictitiously, and any
resemblance to actual persons, living or dead, business establishments,
events, or locales is entirely coincidental.

"The Censor" originally appeared in *Thin Air* 19 (2013); "Undeniable Proof
of the Bigfoot" originally appeared in *The Lindenwood Review* 7 (2017);
"Victories" originally appeared in *Writing Texas* 4 (2016–17); "Clones"
originally appeared in *Steam Ticket: A Third Coast Review* 17 (2014); "The Pub
Runner" originally appeared in *Qwerty* 34 (2015); "The Hero's Embrace"
originally appeared in *Four Chambers* 2 (2014); and "Leaving" originally
appeared in *SLAB* 10 (2015).

In memory of

my mother, KATHLEEN M. DiNUZZO,
and my godmother, KATHERINE J. COSTELLO,
two extraordinary women.

Write with blood, and thou wilt find that blood is spirit.

—FRIEDRICH NIETZSCHE

A short story is like a quick kiss in the dark from a stranger.

—STEPHEN KING

Contents

HOAXES
AND OTHER
STORIES

HOAXES

ACCORDING TO MY NEWS FEED, I died last week. Car accident. Not speeding. Not drinking. Just an accident. I lit out for an evening drive in my 911 Turbo when a Suburban creamed me. Services were held at Grace Episcopal in Oak Park, and my ashes were scattered to the waves off Point Dume. Amber grieved.

On Wednesday, I died again when early-morning curls forced me into a stony outcrop. Hours later, my battered board and battered body washed ashore, nibbled by hungry fish.

Why do I keep dying?

Last year, the daughter of one of Hollywood's biggest producers put me in a feature she had written and was directing. She thought I was cute—a sad yet rebellious James Dean for the twenty-first century with the way I dipped my chin and lifted my eyes, hair blown back, brow creased. The role led to a series of print ads for e-cigs and a run of tequila commercials, which my agent made me do. The feature flopped because—though beautifully shot and accompanied by a melancholic, astral score—the plot proved uneven at best: the cherubic daughter of a heavyweight producer pursues a fledgling actor. But nothing happens, critics complained.

My phone buzzed. "Jackson," I greeted my agent.

"You're dead again."

"I know."

Jackson wanted to issue a press release.

"The last release didn't work," I told him. "Maybe we're just encouraging the pranksters."

Jackson wanted the truth known. "What if a director wants to audition you? What if the tequila people want to pay you for another promotional tour? We can't let prospective employers think you're dead."

"What if I stayed dead for just a little while?"

"Dead is not the role you want to play at this point in your career."

The eight-foot security gate opened and Amber's red 4MATIC Coupe rolled up the driveway. She parked in the shade of the house. "You're not dead!" she said and hugged my neck so hard some vertebrae popped. She slathered me with kisses. "Dead twice in a week. I don't know if I can take this." Amber had the body of her birth mother, Dutch model Gemma Ulin, but the round face of her father, the producer Harvey Brewster.

"Why don't you answer your phone?" Amber playfully smacked my chest. "I knew it was a hoax, but I got scared anyway."

We cobbled together sandwiches and side salads and lunched on the back patio in the warmth of the sun.

"Why do you keep dying?" Amber wanted to know.

I had no idea.

"Maybe it's a good thing," Amber said, setting down her iced tea. "If they keep saying you're dead, then you'll live forever, like a reverse-psychology thing."

My gaze drifted beyond the backyard, down the hill, and over the rooftops to an empty beach and silent sea. The black Pacific loafed against yellow sand. Farther out, some pleasure boats left foamy lines in their wake.

"I guess it's nice to know you're on people's minds," Amber said.

I tapped my phone and showed her my obituary. "I was thinking of framing it," I said. "Hang it above the fireplace maybe."

"Oh, no. Don't. You have to be careful with karma. If you push, karma pushes back."

Amber's parents divorced when she was five. Her mother returned to Holland and was killed by a crazed fan. Amber learned about her mother from back issues of *Time* and *People*. I knew that, if left to continue, this conversation would end with Amber in tears and me kneading her shoulders, so I changed subjects. "Jackson might get me an audition. Some space movie. Big budget. Tom Cruise was mentioned."

Amber brightened, said I could play an astronaut if I left my hair flat.

I leaned back, raising my hands. "First, let's see if I even get an audition."

Amber left bread crusts on her plate and clapped crumbs from her hands. The breeze moved her limp blonde hair. She drew a napkin across her lips, leaving behind a red smear. "I'm going to Japan," Amber said, and the words crashed between us. "The studio guaranteed six weeks, but I'm pushing for nine. I need time to *feel* Tokyo, to sense and hear the city's spirit. I'm already thinking about color schemes and set designs and . . ."

The screenwriter Bob Morton had whipped up an unseemly love story—an older man, a younger woman, expatriates, chance encounters, intrigue. We knew Bob Morton from parties and premieres, a Class A Hollywood prick, though ever resilient. Bob Morton, socially awkward and often jittery, played the typical writer type, a sad kook who thrives in make-believe, a man with no other skill but storytelling. He was drunk or stoned the last time I saw him.

"He's not that Bob Morton anymore," Amber said. "The script is good and Bobby is due."

"How many times has he been to rehab?"

"My dad likes the script, and if done right, this film could be amazing." Amber sipped her iced tea. "I leave at the end of the week."

I returned my gaze to the empty beach below, thought I'd go down there with a blanket and take an afternoon nap.

～

The day before Amber left for Tokyo, I died again—stabbed to death when an assailant already known to L.A. County Sheriffs invaded my home. Apparently, I fought to the end.

Jackson phoned. "Thank God you're okay. I was freaking out."
Jackson paused and I could hear him gulp. "It's been a Valium kind
of morning."

"It's a hoax, Jack. That's all."

"Well, at least your name is out there. No such thing as bad press,
right?" Jackson promised he could get me a spot on a daytime talk
show, so I could explain things, prove I wasn't dead.

"How about auditions, Jack?"

"Nothing yet. But I'm waiting to hear back."

My front gate rolled mechanically on its track and Amber's red
Mercedes appeared. She wasn't alone. Bob Morton had insisted on
tagging along. His presence at my home caught me off guard. He
was never someone I would invite over. "You're alive," he said and
shook my hand. I'd never seen Bob smile before; he had always struck
me as a perpetual depressive.

"The assailant killed your dog," Bob Morton said. "That's devious."

"I don't own a dog, Bob."

"That was a lie, too?"

Amber looped around the front bumper and hugged me. "You're
not dead."

The three of us went to the patio and sat with drinks in hand.

Bob Morton gave the house and yard the once-over. "Tequila and
e-cigs paid for this? Why am I wasting my time with writing?" Bob Morton looked rejuvenated; his face was clean, recently shaved, scoured,
and perfumed. "What I find interesting," Bob said, "was not the death
itself but the method. Hoaxes are often accidents—falls, wrecks, mis-
haps. It's almost a joke by itself to hear that a celebrity, while hik-
ing, literally fell off the side of a mountain or choked on a French
fry or tripped on a garden hose and landed in just such a way. . . . But
you were *murdered*. Nineteen stab wounds is no accident. It's vicious,
personal, and not at all funny." Bob Morton sat a moment, his eyes
gray, disturbed, his lips tense. Then he stirred, clapped, and whooped.
"It's a mad world, brother." I was sure Bob Morton's next screenplay would include a backyard patio scene like this one. I hated that
Bob Morton was right. Celebrity death hoaxes were meant to be

laughable, even campy. They were meant to tease gullible fans, to scam web surfers and fool reporters. But murder by a criminal assailant, by a dog killer: What was funny about that?

"The whole fake death thing is getting pretty lame if you ask me," Amber said. "Maybe I should release a statement through my dad's production company, tell these losers to leave us alone."

Bob Morton, leaning his elbows on the table, unwrapped a cube of nicotine gum and popped it into his mouth. "That's what these tricksters want, Amber." He shrugged and smiled so wide I could see the mint-green knot squished between his molars. I had never before heard Bob Morton say Amber's name. He forced the word into one syllable, bracketed by wild, open-mouth chewing.

Amber's shoulders and eyebrows rose in unison. "But we should do something."

"Ignore it," Bob Morton said, self-satisfied.

Soon, the talk turned to Amber's Tokyo trip.

"Bobby is coming along."

"I'm the distraction," Bob boasted, jerking his thumbs back at himself.

The studio had agreed to allot nine weeks for location shooting, and Amber aimed to return to the States with the film nine-tenths complete.

Bob Morton pulled the gum from his mouth and stuck it to the outside of his drinking glass. "This woman," he said, "is going to bring my words to life."

Even with his new hairstyle and fine threads, Bob Morton would not survive Tokyo. The real, grungy, cantankerous Bob Morton would— after a month of sushi and sake, sleazy karaoke bars, and Japanese strippers—reawaken. I'd bet those odds.

Later, Amber sent Bob to the car and stayed with me, pressing her chest to mine. She told me to call her the second I won the Tom Cruise audition, said we should video chat at least once per week while she was away, and advised me to check the mail because of all the gifts and keepsakes she would send. We hugged and kissed good-bye.

I stood, hands on hips, in the backyard, the sun toasting my head. I swiveled and my eyes ran down the hill to the beach below. Two boys in glistening wetsuits sat with knees up on the beach, their surf-boards like tombstones in the sand. The best waves had left for the day, and soon the beach would be empty again. I wanted to take a book down there and read away the afternoon, but I never did.

∾

A week later Jackson called while I was still in bed.

"Do you want the good news, the bad news, or the awful news?"

"What?"

"You're dead again, and it ain't pretty."

"What happened?"

"Murder-suicide. The tricksters went all out this time, including false statements from a psychiatrist, the county coroner, and a patrol officer. They even posted your suicide note."

"Note?"

"You killed Amber then yourself." Jackson waited, but when I couldn't speak, he said, "And you didn't get the Tom Cruise audition."

I thought I might just stay in bed all day.

"The good news is I'm sending a courier to you with a script," Jackson continued. "Read it with the role of Friend Two in mind."

"I don't want bit parts, Jack. You know I'm ready for more."

"Just read it."

After breakfast I dropped into a patio chair. Down at the beach, dozens of surfers and bodyboarders rode morning curls. I checked my phone and read the latest about my murder-suicide hoax. Sup-posedly, I had roamed Sunset Boulevard in my 911 Turbo and scooped up a blonde Latvian hooker going by the name of Patrijya. Alcohol followed. Drugs followed. Sex followed. Amber caught us. I killed Amber and, after several leaps from the staircase, snapped my own neck with a noose. I was found pants-less. The Latvian sold her story to 20/20.

∾

The intercom buzzed. "Mr. Brewster to see you, sir." The gate rolled back and a silver Bentley rolled forward. Arnold, Harvey Brewster's right-hand man, sprang from the driver's seat and held open the rear door. Harvey Brewster dressed like an earl on safari, in khaki jacket and pants, a diamond-blue ascot ringed his neck and matched his crown-folded pocket square. He wore a full, pecan-brown beard, graying at the chin and sideburns, and still had enough hair to sweep across his head.

I brought him into the backyard, offered him a drink and a seat at the patio table.

Brewster waved me to him. "How about a stroll?"

Decades ago, Harvey Brewster had been tagged a film auteur. Brewster had worked with Brando and Sinatra, with Pacino and De Niro. He had won three Oscars, a crate-load of BAFTAs, and more than one Palme d'Or from Cannes. Though still a producer, Brewster quit directing twenty-five years ago after a string of high-concept box office flops. The divorce came next, followed by Gemma's murder. Brewster retreated from the public eye and raised Amber. And all the while, he could still get any picture made.

I paled in comparison to Brewster's portly three hundred and fifty pounds. We walked down the patio steps toward the swimming pool, gout shortening his stride. The dreamy blue water caught and reflected the sunshine. "I'm headed to the ranch," Brewster said and laid a heavy arm on my shoulder. "Thought I'd pay a visit."

I had always been careful to stay in Brewster's good graces. I wanted him to like me, not because of his Hollywood stature but because I might one day need to ask his permission.

"I don't like annoyances, son, and these hoaxes are an annoyance. Why don't we release a statement and notify the police?"

I assured Brewster that the clowns would get bored soon enough and move on to someone else, that no one would remember the hoaxes a month from now.

Back at the Bentley, Brewster said he had seen my tequila commercials. "Acting is failure broken by momentary success. Be smart in the roles you play and merciless in your portrayals. *Be* the thing."

I shook his meaty hand through the open car window, thanked him for the visit and the advice. Before the gate shut, a young man in a loud red helmet and tinted riding goggles jerked his scooter to a stop at my feet and thrust a package at me. "Sign, please." I scribbled my name and the courier sped off. I tore open the package and out slid a screenplay and a note from Jackson. "Read for Friend Two. Call me when you're done. Jack."

Before I could get comfortable, Amber called from Tokyo. She had heard about the murder-suicide hoax, wanted me to call the police. "We need to arrest these lame-wads." While Amber vented, I wandered the backyard. It had been her idea that Harvey Brewster pay me a visit. At the beach below, a pair of surfers exited the water and packed to leave. I thought I might take Jackson's script down there. But Amber kept on, blathering about hoaxes and the Tokyo shoot and Bob Morton.

I went to bed early but couldn't sleep, couldn't read, either. I found headphones in the bedside drawer and listened to Tibetan meditation music, hoping it would put me to sleep. I worried that with the new day might also come another hoax. *Be the thing*, Harvey Brewster kept saying in my head. *Annoyances won't do, son.* I imagined an audition where the filmmakers cared more about the hoaxes than my acting chops.

~

All morning I stayed away from my computer and the TV and shut off my phone. I didn't want to know what the hoaxers were posting, blogging, and tweeting about me. I didn't want to know what gruesome lies they had devised. Instead, I took a cup of steaming black tea onto the back patio, wrapped my bathrobe around my bare legs, and wished for a statewide power failure. Later, I traversed the lawn to the edge of the property and studied the sunrise surfers enjoying the last rolls of high tide. Still, an anxiousness persisted in me, came as a low shiver to my arms, legs, and shoulders. I struggled through a plate of scrambled eggs and toast, then planted myself in a patio chair and turned back the first page of the script. I didn't allow myself to stop reading until I reached the end.

The script was okay, not great; it made sense, which can't be said for all movie scripts, and sure, I could play Friend Two. In fact, I thought Friend Two might have been written solely for me and knew I could be a scene-stealer. I pictured moviegoers leaving the theater, saying, "The guy who played Friend Two . . . wow, just . . . wow." Of course, I could play Friend One, as well. Really, I could play the lead, Hunter Brawn, a sedate husband and father who plays by the rules until mobsters destroy his family, torch his home, crash his sedan, and steal his dog. Powered by his own brand of justice, Hunter Brawn singlehandedly takes down the crime syndicate. Yeah, I could play that role.

I called Jack. "What about the lead? Tell them"—I deepened my voice—"I *am* Hunter Brawn."

"They want you for Friend Two."

We argued awhile until Jackson agreed to express my sincere interest in auditioning for the lead.

"Anything else new?" I asked.

"Hoaxes, you mean? Nope."

Each day without a hoax felt better than the previous day. I sipped tea in my bathrobe and waited for Jackson's call. Amber and I talked by video or phone a few times but never for very long; her shooting schedule was impossibly demanding, and Bob Morton was always getting in the way.

Jackson called. "No-go on the lead, but you got Friend Two. You don't even have to audition. What should I tell them?"

I wanted to protest, to prove to those producers and that director that I was ready to lead a movie, that I could *be* Hunter Brawn, hero. I was ready for the challenge.

"What should I tell them?"

"Tell them I'll take Friend Two," I said unhappily.

Jackson assured me I'd made the right choice, said I should be glad for the work and the paycheck. Before he hung up, he asked if I had heard the news.

"No."

"Then you better turn on the TV."

In just the last hour raw video surfaced of Bob Morton in Tokyo. After trashing his hotel room, Bob entered the swank lobby, shoving guests and porters, smashing ceramic vases, toppling statues. He wore a trench coat over blue boxers and black socks, his hair a chaotic tangle. Two and then three hotel security guards wrestled Bob to the ground. He kicked and squirmed and vomited across the marble floor. One of the guards hit the sludge, landed hard, grabbing his elbow, writhing in pain, slathered in puke. Two more security guards joined the fight. Bob Morton screamed Japanese gibberish; he growled, he spat, he threatened to deck anyone who touched him. By now, the guards had gotten Bob onto his belly, planted their knees in his back, and cuffed him. The video clip ended with the guards muscling Bob to the exit while Bob promised lawsuits.

I turned off the TV when my phone rang. "He's gone bonkers!" Amber boomed on the line. "He flipped out!" I told Amber I'd just seen the news. "That's not half of it," she said. Before the hotel lobby fiasco, Bob Morton had spent days shuttling between Tokyo strip clubs and exotic massage parlors. Along the way, Bob had ingested powders, pills, and liquids, paid strippers to dance privately in his hotel room, to have sex with him, with each other. "Oh, and the best part," Amber added, "Bob took a hammer to our set. Do you know how much time and money it will cost to rebuild all of the interiors?" Amber released a warbling sob. "The mayor of Tokyo is considering kicking us out of the country, and the studio is threatening to pull the plug. I . . ."

The next day Bob Morton was expelled from Japan with a bill for restitution. He landed at SFO and entered an extended-stay clinic in Modesto. Harvey Brewster swooped in with his influence and his money and became lead producer for his daughter's film. Sets were rebuilt, filming continued.

A day later, the phone rang, a number I didn't recognize.

"Hello."

"You're going to die," the gruff voice said.

"Who is this?"

"Someone is going to hop over your fence, creep into the house while you sleep, snap your dog's neck, then stab you to death."

I wrote down the caller's number, so that when I called the police, they'd have a lead.

"What do you think about that?" The caller wheezed laughter.

"I don't have a dog, asshole, and that hoax has already been pulled. Can't you even be original?"

The laughter crescendoed then ground to a stop. "It's me, Bob Morton. I had you fooled, didn't I?" Bob was still in Modesto, still in rehab, still a Class A Hollywood prick. "We get phone privileges for ten minutes per day and I already called my mom and dad." Bob laughed anew, then whispered: "I'm still high, brother. There are more drugs inside than outside."

Bob wouldn't let me go.

"You know about Tokyo, don't you?"

"You went bonkers, Bob."

"Amber and I slept together."

I remained unfazed. This might have been another hoax, and I wouldn't give Bob the satisfaction of rousing my emotions. "You don't believe me," he said. "We didn't plan it, and we really didn't enjoy it." Bob's tone changed, hollowed by remorse. "It just happened."

"I have to go, Bob. Enjoy rehab."

"Wish me luck," he said. "At midnight, I'm breaking out of this place."

"Good luck, Bob," I said and immediately placed a call to the clinic, tipping off the head of security.

I tried to forget about Bob and Amber but couldn't. Amber called, crying again, and confessed to a one-night stand with Bob Morton. "I was excited and a little drunk, and then it was done. I'm sorry."

I didn't know what to say.

"Are we okay?" Amber asked.

I died that day. On set. I hit my mark just as a lighting rig collapsed. Instant death. Producers and crew mourned. Production halted until a replacement for Friend Two could be found.

~

What if I stayed dead for just a little while longer?

I unfurled a beach blanket and planted myself cross-legged in the warm sand. The grains glowed gold and copper, amber and saffron, but, digging my fingers deep, I felt the cool beneath the surface, dense with moisture. Behind me and high above, stood my house, white and cube-like in design with elongated windows, impressive when set against the green sage scrub of a California hillside.

Surfers in black wetsuits with fluorescent-colored limbs moved forward and backward through the water. Two young men sat astride their boards in the calm behind the curls. They bobbed like toy boats, talked animatedly, gestured occasionally. Intermittent swells encroached from the horizon. The young men studied each wave and, when a suitable specimen approached, paddled into position. Seamlessly, the water bulged and heaved forward, pregnant, and the young men snapped from their bellies onto their feet, legs spread, arms extended winglike. They angled their waxed blades, crouching as the ocean curved over their backs and surrounded them in a cylinder of salt-water. And at their heels, the cylinder collapsed, always an instant too late. They rode the waves until nothing remained, until momentum died and the barmy, frothing ocean again flattened, and they fell back to their bellies.

The young woman with them took a different approach. While her male counterparts selected only the best waves, the young woman rode every swell she could, quantity over quality. She measured the mood and language of every ripple, great and small, and though she wiped out often, she always bobbed back to the surface with a flick of her head and a smile on her face.

A swell of sleep rose in me, and rather than take my board to the water, I lay back on the blanket and promptly fell asleep. When I woke, the shadows had moved, the sun too; even the ocean had shifted upon the shore. The sky had paled and the clouds scattered; the world itself awoke anew. Bob Morton, the crackpot screenwriter, had slept with Amber, a woman I used to love, one who now felt farther from me than Tokyo from Hollywood by a million miles.

I sat up, hoping to wash away my exhaustion. The male surfers stood out by the road loading their boards into the back of a Honda, peeling off their wetsuits, leaving their torsos bare. The young woman remained in the water, her ponytail whipping behind her like the tail of a drenched cat. She caught a sizeable wave, thrived a moment until the crumbling tube engulfed her. She bobbed to the surface all smiles.

The young woman trudged from the surf, board in hand, knocking water from her ears. She plodded through the sand to meet her pals, and they drove off together.

Amber Brewster died after the premiere of her Bob Morton–scripted film. Accidental overdose. Her father found her. He grieved. The hoax lasted just long enough for her movie and her prestige to die, too, and she drifted back under her father's umbrella. And Amber and I, we simply ended. Like a collapsed wave. Like an instant death. Like a hoax.

THE STORM

MICKEY SWAYED IN AN oak tree's uppermost branches, listening to John Waite's "Missing You" on his handheld radio. He could see balls nesting in the rain gutters at the top of the house. He could see the entire backyard: the patio, the sandbox, the jungle gym, and his mother's pitiful garden. Mickey spat a high, arcing gob into his mother's wilting tomato plants. From the back porch Aaron called to Mickey, and the boy rappelled out of the tree and followed his big brother into the house.

Since forever, a sizeable crack split the basement's cement floor, so that even during the lightest rains, black water seeped from the crack and formed nasty pools around the basement. The brothers stepped carefully, avoiding the puddles. Mold bloomed in the corners and climbed the bare, cinderblock walls, and lightbulbs hung overhead, throwing lousy yellow light about the windowless space. The boys' father had installed the lights but quit before fully refurbishing the basement, just as he had quit the family when Mickey was seven years old. Mickey didn't miss his father, though. He didn't miss the scoldings, the orders to do this or stop doing that, and he definitely did not miss the criticisms or outright punishments for ticking off his father.

A pool table without cue sticks or balls filled the basement. Their father had left the old thing behind to rot in this neglected part of the house. Aaron pointed to the pool table. "Our ship," he said. "Hurry! We are surrounded by hungry sharks." The boys leaped atop the worn, green felt. Aaron piloted the pretend vessel and directed Mickey to "trim the sails," whatever that meant. Together, the brothers sailed the open sea, cresting waves and sliding into watery valleys.

"How will we get off?" Mickey asked, growing bored.

Aaron shrugged. Imaginary hammerheads, great whites, and ragged-tooth sharks jammed the space between the pool table and the stairs. "I have an idea," Aaron said. "If we distract the sharks and if we are fast enough, we could reach the stairs before getting chomped." But one boy would have to play bait while the other raced to safety. "Hang your leg over the side," Aaron said to Mickey.

"No way. They'll bite me."

"Do it, but do it quick," Aaron said, "and I'll break for the stairs."

Mickey peered overboard and saw not the cracked basement floor, not icky puddles, but a churning, frosty ocean with waves swelling and slamming the hull and salty mist spraying his face. Large, dark shapes with mouths like caves and teeth like sword tips slithered among the waves.

"Do it," Aaron yelled. "Now!"

Adrenaline flooded Mickey's chest. Kneeling at the edge of the pool table, he dropped one leg over the side. "Go," he called, sharks already investigating his submerged limb. With one snap, a shark could take Mickey's entire leg. How would he run to the stairs then? How would he climb trees or fences or ride a bicycle? "Go, Aaron!"

Aaron leaped from the pool table and ran, hurdling the crack in the floor, dodging puddles and vicious sharks. He reached the stairs safely and turned back. Mickey had already yanked his leg out of the water. "Now you," Aaron said to his brother. "Your turn."

Having been fooled once, the sharks showed an increased aggression, clapping their jaws, whipping their tail fins, and ramming the ship's hull. "No way," Mickey said. "I'll wait until the sharks leave."

"There's no time. The ship is sinking."

"No, it's not."

"It is. Look."

Aaron was right. Saltwater gushed between damaged wooden planks.

"I can repair the leaks," Mickey said and worked his hands over the green felt.

"No," Aaron corrected. "The fixes have failed. Jump or get eaten."

Mickey wanted to protest, but when he looked at the ship's condition, he knew the truth.

"You have no choice. Jump, Mickey!"

Seawater poured onto the ship, and every second the sharks drew closer. Mickey had to act. He scrambled to the pool table's edge, jumped, and sprinted to the stairs. Only, when he arrived on the bottom step, Aaron was gone. And an instant later, the basement lights winked out.

Aaron had been scheming from the start. His invitation to play in the basement had always been a trick, a plan to frighten Mickey.

The sea rose and overtook Mickey on the staircase, and with the water came enraged sharks. The terrible-tooth monsters prowled after Mickey, who scrabbled from step to step in search of higher ground, trying to reach the basement door, bashing his kneecap along the way and jamming some fingers as he fumbled in the dark. Mickey stretched out an arm and caught the doorknob and for a brief instant thought he would escape before the sharks made lunch of him. But the door was locked, and somewhere on the other side of the door, Aaron was cackling.

"Mom!" Mickey screamed and thumped a fist against the basement door. "I don't want to play anymore." Despite the dark, he could see the sharks' crazy black eyes, the glowing razor-teeth; he could even see the merciless hunger driving these savage creatures to him. He bellowed and hammered the door again, and Aaron went on laughing, howling. "Don't look, Mickey. You don't want to see the *thing* right behind you," Aaron called through the door.

A creature's hot, salty breath tickled Mickey's neck, and teeth tugged his flesh. His heart thudded; his lungs pumped; his imagination overpowered him. He did not want to be ground between molars or shredded and consumed piece by piece. Mickey cowered in the dark, waiting to die, too terrified to do anything but shiver, and he remained like that until he heard the faint click of the lock. Exhausted by fear,

Mickey unfurled himself and turned the doorknob. The door swung back and daylight stung his eyes. Aaron laughed and pointed at Mickey, called him a baby. Mickey, still in shock, said nothing but secretly threatened revenge.

When their mother came home, Mickey told her what had happened, that Aaron had tricked him, had shut off the lights and locked the basement door, that giant, monster sharks had nearly devoured him alive.

"Really?" his mother said, her irksome tone matching the look in her eyes. "Don't I have enough stress?"

"Don't believe him, Mom," Aaron said from the opposite side of the kitchen.

"But it's true," Mickey objected.

"I don't care what's true," his mother said.

"But you have to punish him."

"All I want right now is silence and peace." She pulled a rosé bottle from the paper bag cradled in one arm, poured a glass, and sat with her back to her boys. "Leave me alone."

Mickey seethed all afternoon and all night. Aaron had abused him and his mother had denied him justice. The anger that festered within Mickey devolved into outright hatred by the next morning. If he could not get justice, Mickey would make his brother and mother regret their behavior. He would make them miss him, make them ache with longing and weep with remorse and self-condemnation. He would run away. The brilliant idea flourished inside of him, followed by this thought: Had his father left because he had been victimized, too?

The next morning, Mickey stealthily backed Aaron's shiny bicycle out of the garage, pulled on his backpack, and coasted down the driveway. The houses on Red Oak irritated Mickey. He needed to escape the block, the neighborhood, the entire town, needed to find a place his brother and mother would never look.

Cool air passed over Mickey as he pedaled, and gray clouds moved above, turning and twisting, contorting and distorting. Had his mother and brother noticed his absence yet? Were they already searching for him, calling his name, checking his bedroom, scouring the backyard treetops? Mickey listened for his mother's voice on the wind but heard nothing. Rising out of his seat, he pedaled harder, pumping his legs and starting his heart racing. Should he have left a note for them to find? His father had left no note.

Mickey turned off of Red Oak, rode clear out of the neighborhood and out of town. He rode until he encountered foreign street signs and alien storefronts. The sun appeared, warming Mickey's crown for a quick moment before swirling clouds swallowed the light. No matter how fast he pedaled, Mickey could not outdistance the gathering storm clouds.

As Mickey whizzed around a street corner, a crack of thunder tore across the sky, and the roads became nearly deserted. Plump, slow-falling raindrops splattered Mickey's hands and forearms, his shoulders and back, but he stayed relatively dry and pedaled aggressively to the top of an inclining road. The wind pushed back his hair, and the rainfall increased. Far ahead, a row of shops promised shelter from the rain. "Sorry, We're Closed" signs hung in all three shop windows, but Mickey didn't care. He rolled to a stop under a wide green awning and shook raindrops from his bangs. He recognized one of the shops—a greeting card and knickknack store he had visited once before. He and his mother had come to the store from Grandma's house. The old woman had been ill but was improving, and during good-byes, Grandma had pushed folded bills into Mickey's hand. His mother had stayed in the car while Mickey entered the store and bought packs of baseball cards, more for the gum than for the cards themselves. The memory comforted Mickey, and he held onto it until thunder clapped and lightning flashed. Was his father holding on to any memories?

Mickey pulled Aaron's bicycle deeper under the awning, leaning it against the store's façade. Whirling gray clouds collided overhead, sparking more lightning. Mickey sat on a narrow, brick window ledge. He shrugged off his backpack, pulled the zipper, and dug out a sloppy peanut butter and jelly sandwich sealed in plastic. Though quite hungry, Mickey stopped himself from eating more than a few bites. Who knew how long the rain might last? Who knew from where his next meal might come? He was on his own now and had to be smart. He returned the sandwich to the backpack.

The rain continued, falling harder and faster by the minute; parking lot puddles shimmered and danced and swelled. Sometimes, crooked fingers of lightning stretched from one black cloud to another. Infrequently, an automobile with headlights blazing and wipers whipping passed in a spray of rainwater. Mickey thought about his mother and brother at home. Were they calling his name, wondering where he'd gone off to? Had they noticed the missing bicycle and made the connection? Were they blaming themselves for his disappearance? Was his mother blabbing to cops, admitting that she had mistreated her boy? Had Aaron confessed to being a scheming older brother and superb tormentor? Were they blaming themselves for being rotten people? Had his father shared similar thoughts: Am I missed? Do these bastards regret their actions?

Mickey studied the hard-driving rain with the belief that the harder it poured the sooner the storm would end. But an hour later, the parking lot puddles had multiplied and tiny rivers quickly overwhelmed a lone storm drain. Farther away, water deluged the sidewalks and flooded the roadway, and in all that water, he spotted hungry sharks prowling for easy food.

At the end of the row of shops, rainwater from the awning streamed into a fifteen-gallon wine-barrel flowerpot. Mickey peered over the lip; if there had been daisies or tulips or mums there, they had long since drowned. Behind Mickey, the gusting wind sent Aaron's bicycle crashing onto its side. Ever-increasing thunder and lightning played like an enraged choir. The storm boomed fury and poured anger and showed no hint of ending. Could a storm rage forever?

Mickey fished his handheld radio out of his backpack. Static played on every station until he switched the band and, adjusting the dial carefully, caught a signal. A serious-sounding man was saying, "Again, this is an extreme weather emergency. Residents are advised to stay indoors, stay off roads, and stay away from windows. We are in for a rough afternoon."

The overhead awning—thick canvas stretched over a metal frame—
rattled. A canvas strip had torn loose and flapped wildly. The wind
forced rain under the awning, and Mickey retreated into the shop's
recessed doorway. Rainwater crested the walkway and snaked toward
Mickey's sneakers.

His mother and Aaron must have been ransacking the house by
now, searching the garage and basement, pawing through closets, peering under bed frames. She must have interrogated Aaron, demanded
answers from him, and concluded, "Well, he didn't just *leave*. Who
would leave during such a terrible storm?" Her anger would soon turn
to despair and then to desperation. She and Aaron would destroy the
house in search of him. They'd flip furniture and tear clothes from
hangers; they would search all the places they had already searched.
And after desperation, his mother and Aaron would experience a
deep, potent, scarring sorrow, and they would wallow in the misery
they had created. Had they been so miserable when his father left?

Some hours later, Mickey decided that his mother and brother
had suffered enough. If the rain just eased a bit and the flooding sub-
sided, he could ride home. He had ridden in rain before but never
a storm, never with such limited visibility and frequent lightning
strikes, never with sharks waiting in ambush. In the last twenty minutes only one vehicle passed, a slow-moving truck with flashing
orange lights and Public Works Dept. painted on the door. Raindrops
had sparkled in the truck's high beams. With such dreadful conditions, Mickey would have to wait. Had a similar stubborn storm kept
his father from returning?

Hunger drove Mickey into his backpack. He swallowed a few more
bites of his sandwich and saved the rest. Wind whipped beneath the
awning, trying to dislodge the covering and turn it into a massive,
deranged kite. The wind blew so hard that Mickey thought *he* would
become the kite that flew away. The radio crackled with new and terrible news: Tornadoes had been spotted and confirmed. Mickey turned
his eyes to the sky. The clouds there drooped and sagged toward the
ground, twisting, funneling. The wind and rain accelerated, and puddles pinned Mickey against the store's façade. He crouched in the

doorway, trying to make himself a dense, compact anchor. The awning clattered unceasingly now, the canvas tear widening. Branches, torn from trees, slid like hockey sticks across the drenched parking lot. Mickey clutched the doorknob with two hands, mooring himself. Thunder boomed and lightning flashed, and the wine-barrel flower-pot capsized, sending a wave over the walkway and soaking Mickey's sneakers and socks. Cold moisture squished between his toes. In the tide of spilled water, three yellow daisies sailed past, their exposed, veiny roots trailing after. The parking lot became a raging sea, and the sharks there roiled and snapped, starved for fresh meat.

The canvas awning puffed with air, lifted, and crashed back at a cocked angle. The more the canvas shredded, the more rain sprayed Mickey, and soon his clothes turned wet and cold. If he died in the storm, how would his mother and brother find him? Had death kept his father from returning home all these years? The thought shocked Mickey. He did not want to die, did not want to hurt his family any longer. He tucked his chin against his chest, shut his eyes, redoubled his grip on the doorknob, and would not surrender to the storm. Home beckoned.

Mickey didn't need any weather forecasters to tell him that the storm had passed. The ever so subtle changes in wind and rain, clouds and barometric pressure signaled the end. Puddles turned placid, and the trees across the street straightened. The rainfall lightened, lightened, and ceased, and the storm clouds fragmented and dissipated and gave way to cheery white clouds, and when the pools of water receded, the sharks vanished. Mickey waited until he saw vehicles on the road again before he released his grip on the doorknob.

As he biked through the wet streets, Mickey refined the story he would tell: He'd swear he was at a friend's house playing video games, would say he had hardly noticed the storm. He'd apologize but claim he had told his mother his plans. He'd promise to act more responsibly in the future.

Mickey coasted down Red Oak, passing leaf- and branch-littered lawns, dodging garbage cans and lids strewn across the roadway. He entered through the garage's side door, parked Aaron's bike against the wall, and removed his soggy sneakers and socks before quietly entering the house. He followed the sound of the TV to the living room, where his mother and Aaron sat on the couch watching Superman save Richard Pryor from himself.

"Hi," Mickey said and was ignored. He tried again. "What are you doing?"

"What do you think we're doing?" Aaron said, as cantankerous as ever. "Don't block the TV."

Mickey crossed the living room on the way to his bedroom to change into dry clothes. His mother and brother had not noticed his soggy appearance, had not noticed his absence. They didn't know he had run away and been caught in a nasty storm, and they did not miss him. Mickey peeled off his wet clothes and collapsed naked onto his bed, tears flooding his eyes. Had they ever missed his father? Mickey certainly did. He missed his father more than ever.

VALENTINA

DAVE HUSTLED BACK AND FORTH from the rental truck to his new apartment, trying to finish unloading before the sun came over the rooftops and the heat turned dangerous. A teenaged girl lounged on a nearby hammock, surrounded by and presiding over children about ages five to eleven. Each time Dave passed, lugging a box or side table, a lamp or chair, the children chirped Spanish and giggled sharply, mockingly. Only the girl on the hammock, arms tucked behind her head, remained composed.

Dave maneuvered the kitchen table through the doorway, careful not to scuff the freshly painted walls, and stood in his new living room. "I'm Valentina. Who are you?" the girl from the hammock asked as she entered Dave's apartment, scanning the corners of the room and speaking an accented English. "Where's Mrs. Muñez? She used to let me feed her cats." Valentina reflected a moment. "I guess she's gone."

While struggling to find a spot for the table, Dave introduced himself.

"Mrs. Muñez put the TV and couch over there. The table goes here." Valentina turned. "And that was where Luna coughed up a hairball like this." She made a fist. "It was disgusting." Valentina followed Dave out to the truck, asking, "Why are you here?"

"I've been asking myself that same question for the last eight hundred miles." Valentina's face showed confusion. "I got a job here, so I'm here," Dave said. "But I'm not sure this was a good idea."

"Why?"

Dave was happy for the company—it had been a lonely, stressful eight hundred miles—yet he was skeptical of the girl's inquiries. Some kids couldn't be trusted. When Dave was fifteen, he had been a practiced beggar, thief, and vandal. For all he knew Valentina could be a kleptomaniac con artist with daddy issues.

Valentina stood by as Dave fought the loveseat out of the truck and prepared for the final haul.

"Stand back," he warned.

Arms crossed, Valentina didn't budge. "You're going to lift that by yourself?"

"I'm stronger than I look." He meant it as a joke, but Valentina whistled and the children she was tending ran over to spectate. They gasped as he heaved, his legs quivering. He groaned and grunted and muscled the loveseat through the doorframe, skinning his knuckles in the process. The children cheered.

When it was time to return the truck, Valentina climbed into the passenger seat. "Do you got any money?"

"Where are your parents? Wouldn't your dad be upset to find you in a stranger's truck?"

"You don't know my dad."

Maybe Valentina was not a con artist but a decoy, sent to distract Dave while some scumbags forced the lock and robbed his new place. Was all this friendliness a scheme to cheat the outsider?

Valentina wouldn't get out and Dave wouldn't move the truck. They sat in a stalemate until one of the kids, a girl about seven years old, bloodied her knee running in the parking lot and began to cry. Her whimpering brought Valentina. "Haven't I told you the parking lot is dangerous?" she told the girl. While Valentina tended to the child, Dave started the rental truck and drove away.

～

Dave didn't have to report to work until the following week and planned to ease into his new surroundings. But, because of the time zone change, he woke early, his neck and back stiff from all the lifting and lugging. His wrist ached as he opened the door and found Valentina waiting. "Good morning," she said. "You look like shit."

"Thanks. That's kind of you."

He tried to slip past her, but she blocked the way. "Do you want to hang out? I'm not doing anything today. I could give you a tour." Valentina shielded her eyes from the early sunlight, and for the first time Dave noted the green specks mixed into her brown irises. Many sunny days had turned her face and limbs the color of a roasted turkey. She wore unlaced high-tops and shorts cut from discarded denim. Scarred knees evinced her toughness, bespoke experience, and an oversized T-shirt coated with dirt and dark stains hung off one shoulder. Valentina's waist-long brown hair demanded a wash and a comb-through. The frizzy ends, once bleach blonde, were now dull mustard. Her face needed scrubbing with a soapy brush.

"We'll hang out later," Dave said.

Valentina trailed him to the parking lot. "This is your car? Boring."

"At least it gets me where I want to go."

Valentina asked to drive it; Dave refused. "Once I get my license," she said, "I'm going to buy a sports car, something fast and uncatchable."

~

Dave returned an hour later. He carried shopping bags into the apartment and set them down in the tiny kitchen. When he went back to the car for the remaining bags, Valentina already had them. "What are you doing?" He accused more than asked, figuring the girl had swiped something, that if he looked under her shirt or in her back pocket, he'd find what didn't belong to her.

"I'm helping," she said and smiled. The smile reminded Dave that Valentina was still a child. Her teeth, though caked with plaque, were big and new, ready for a lifetime of chewing, and her cheeks plumped with vigor. At the same time, disproportionately long legs signaled burgeoning womanhood.

"Thanks, Val, but allow me." Dave took the bags from her. If any items were missing, he'd confront her. For now, though, she was innocent.

Valentina used both hands to close the trunk. She snatched Dave's keys, unlocked and held open the apartment door, and closed it after he entered. "You should really put your TV where Mrs. Muñez had it, your couch, too. I'm not used to it any other way." Dave placed perishables in the refrigerator, nonperishables in the cabinets, all the while keeping watch on Valentina. He caught her nosing around the bedroom door. "Get out of there."

She shuddered and backed away, saying, "Don't blow your lid, Dave. I was just looking."

Casing, plotting, scheming were more like it.

When he hinted that Valentina should leave, she said, "What about your tour?"

Afraid of another stalemate, Dave followed Valentina outside. She pointed past the grill and hammocks where he had first seen her to an identical apartment building. "I live there, on the first floor. A two-bedroom. It's okay." Valentina said she lived with Marco and Silvia, her parents. "And I have brothers and sisters back home."

"Where's home?"

"Mexico. Once we get enough money, we'll bring them over."

Valentina seemed so comfortable with Dave that he thought she might hold his hand, so he buried his hands deep in his pockets. She guided him between two other buildings, told a story for each. "I was in love with a boy named Joey in that building. He went to Oklahoma because his parents divorced. But he promised to visit me when he learned how to drive. And Mr. Renner lived in that building with his pit bull, Thunder. Thunder hated everyone. One day Mr. Renner fell over and never got up. An ambulance took him away, and two dog catchers took Thunder away. Now somebody else lives there."

Six washers lined the left wall of the laundry room and six dryers the right wall. A folding table stood beside a trash bin and lint balls scattered to the corners. The room smelled of Lilac Ocean detergent. Valentina opened the door to leave and the wind blew back her hair, exposing a tender, unwashed neck, and pulsing, blue jugular. At that moment—with the sun slashing across her body, the draft in her hair, her long legs—she was a lady, sure of herself, leading her servant through the kingdom. As she bounded down the steps, Dave following, Valentina reached back and caught his hand. Dave couldn't say when he had taken his hands from his pockets or why he held on. Her palm was cool, small, not as delicate as one might expect, a testament to her roughhousing and soccer playing. She took him to the fitness center. The lights were off, but the sun slipped through gaps in the blinds. A ceiling fan spun lazily and with little effect. The cramped, dark room contained two archaic treadmills, two workout benches, and a handful of rusty, misshapen dumbbells. The mirrored walls created an illusion of space that did not really exist. "Fitness center," Dave said. "It's more like a fitness closet."

They each mounted a treadmill, and Valentina showed Dave how to start the belt. The machines cranked to life, grumbling and squeaking. Valentina grinned. "This is fun, right, Dave?"

Valentina said she had lived at the complex for four years, said she easily made friends but could never keep them because people didn't live in a dump any longer than necessary.

"Why have you stayed?"

"Marco, my dad, says it's temporary. He says we're gonna buy a house and bring my brothers and sisters here. But then something happens. Marco leases a new truck or makes some dumb bets or work dries up. Something always happens and we have to start all over again. Sometimes I think Marco likes the way things are. Not me."

Valentina bragged that she was the only kid from the complex who didn't attend school. School, she said, never felt right. "My first year in America, I went to school and learned English, but after that, school got boring, so I just stopped going."

"Don't you need an education?"

Valentina shrugged. "I tell people I want to be a dentist and that makes them feel good. The truth"—Valentina slowed the treadmill and leaned close—"the truth is I won't say what I really want because people will try to stop me. Hope is flimsy enough."

By the time they had walked a mile, the exuberant Valentina returned. She bounced off the treadmill. The back door to the fitness center led them to the pool, where an iron-and-wood fence surrounded the glimmering oval on which floated a lone ring buoy. A white sign with red lettering hung on the gate: "No lifeguard. Swim at your own risk. Pool closes at 10 p.m." Valentina stared at the glinting surface.

"Want to go in?" Dave asked, bending to touch the water.

"I can't swim. And, anyway, I hate bathing suits."

She brought Dave to the parking lot, a long strip of blacktop that circled the complex. Most of the parking spaces were empty. Soggy, leaking garbage bags overflowed the dumpsters, and all kinds of refuse—wrappers, napkins, plastic bottles—littered the lot. "This is a dangerous place," Valentina said, toeing the chipped spout of a beer bottle, nudging it away from the tires of Dave's car. "You could get hurt in a parking lot like this."

∼

Dave rolled in a little before 6 p.m., easing his car over each speed bump. Already men in dirty blue jeans and construction boots gathered beside their vehicles, watching, waiting, their grim faces a patchwork of bold distrust and blatant animosity. Dave glared back. He had already noticed that all types of men congregated in the complex's parking lot at night. They huddled at truck tailgates, squatted on cement parking curbs, or lounged in the front seats of jalopies, drinking, smoking, loitering, seeking relief from their despicable lives. As Dave drove toward his building, a young man stepped from between two parked cars, hiding what looked like a screwdriver and pliers behind the legs of his baggy shorts. The scumbag—Was he attempting to steal a car?—was not more than a foot from Dave's window. They swapped venomous stares, and Dave thought, if something happens, I'll have to fight dirty to survive.

After Dave parked, as he made his way across the lot, he spotted kids with a soccer ball. The children, none more than ten or twelve, sweat-slicked and grimy, cursed and teased each other. Mostly boys, they carried in their plump, dark faces the furiousness of rabid beasts, eager to kick and bite and scratch, as likely to attack an outsider as to turn on and destroy each other. Valentina blazed around the corner of a building, her now-dyed-pink hair flapping behind in long waves.

"Who was it?" she said. "Tell me. Point him out." She was talking to a particular girl, who flinched when Valentina grabbed her. "Tell me who, Mariella. Tell me now, Mariella."

Stiffly, Mariella raised her arm. "José," she said, indicating a pre-teen who wore a Real Madrid jersey, his flesh burned brown, his hair shaved and spiked into a diffuse mohawk.

Panicked, José bolted but only made two strides before Valentina pounced and dragged him face down into the grass.

The others circled. Valentina pinned José and batted the back of his head. The boy tried to dislodge her, tried to stand, but without success. "Shut up. Shut up!" Valentina said as José began to cry and call for his mom. She took fists of his hair and cranked back his head. The boy looked like a beached seal made to perform tricks. "Slut?" Valentina said, the word slithering out of her mouth. "Is that it, a slut?" José begged for mercy. Two other boys moved to intervene, but Valentina's menacing glare stopped them.

"You're not," José said. "You're not, Val. No way."

Valentina drove her fist into the boy's lower back. He jerked and cried. She punched the side of his neck, then, leaning close to his ear, said, "And what's wrong with being a slut? I'd rather be a slut than a burnt turd like you."

The older kids laughed.

"Sorry, Val. Sorry."

She forced his head into the turf. "If I ever hear you talking crap about me again, you'll be playing soccer with a limp." Valentina punched José again before backing away, her oversized shirt collar exposing a bare shoulder. José squinted as he stood, steadying himself against another boy's shoulder, and brushed grass clippings from his shirt and hair. He hobbled away, muttering profanities.

∾

Though the sun had been down for hours, the heat remained. The apartment felt like a sealed shoebox, and Dave had to get out. He discovered some comfortable chairs on the deck behind the leasing office and relaxed, putting his feet up. Mosquitoes buzzed. Valentina emerged from the dark, wearing the same clothes, the same pink hair. "Is that you, Val?"

She stood on the opposite side of the deck railing, resting her chin on the balustrade, a cell phone encased in neon pink in one hand. She said nothing about her fight with José.

"Aren't your parents wondering where you are?" Dave asked.

"Prob'ly not."

"Will the heat ever end?"

Valentina shrugged. She wanted companionship not conversation.

"I can't take this heat," Dave said.

Valentina boarded the deck, slouched in a chair, and rested her long legs on the wooden railing. The laces of her high-tops dangled. Mosquitoes left red welts on her legs and new abrasions crisscrossed her knees. Her phone chimed. Valentina thumbed back a reply. The messaging continued until Valentina said, "Mariella thinks you're cute, but don't tell her I told you. She trusts me with too many secrets." Valentina wrote a message to Mariella. "I'm telling her you like her only as a friend."

Dave protested against Valentina speaking on his behalf. But the message had been sent.

A trio of young men gathered in the parking lot around a pickup truck, listening to bachata and swigging from dark bottles. Laughter erupted from the group sometimes, their bottles clinking, their raucous Spanish swirling into the night sky.

"Do they even live here?" Dave wondered aloud. "Only scumbags hang out in parking lots."

Valentina said, "You don't want to piss off Melky and his boys. Believe me." Melky had been the screwdriver-and-pliers guy who had given Dave a dirty look as he rolled through the parking lot. Tired of swatting mosquitoes, Dave stood. "Between the heat and those scumbags, I don't know how I'm going to sleep."

"Take a shower, as cold as you can stand it. Then jump into bed. It helps."

Valentina stood, too, and ambled toward the trio in the parking lot, thumbs dancing on her cellphone.

∽

By the time Dave reached the parking lot the next morning, his damp hair had dried and his car was missing, and if he didn't hurry, he'd be late for his first day of work. Dreading the worst, he charged toward the leasing office. On the way, he found Valentina swinging lazily on a hammock, her thin arm pitched over one side. She slowly opened her eyes.

"Did you sleep out here all night?"

She hushed him. "It's too early." Valentina reached beneath the hammock, raised a soda can to her lips, and drank. A line of cola dribbled to her chin. She wiped a bare arm across her mouth. "Dave?" Her knees parted briefly as she rolled toward him. "Got any money?"

Had he not been so rushed, so concerned about his missing car and his first day of work, Dave might have entertained Valentina's silliness. "I have to go," he said.

"The office ain't open till nine."

"My car—"

"It's gone, Dave."

"Was it towed?"

"Stolen."

This had to be a practical joke—make the new tenant sweat and panic, then spring the punchline. Or had Melky and his boys been involved?

"Cars here get swiped all the time, Dave."

"What do you know about it? Who took my car?"

She looked away and looked back. "I don't know. Now, let me sleep." Her eyelids drooped, her body sagged, and she stank of alcohol. What had happened during the night? What did Valentina become?

He wanted to interrogate her but knew he'd get nothing from the lush until she sobered. He raced to the leasing office anyway, sweat prickling his brow. The door was locked, the lights dark. Dave dialed his boss's number. He would explain the situation, promise to get a cab and get to the office as soon as he filed a police report. Only, before the call connected, Dave spotted his car parked in the fire zone, half hidden by a green dumpster. He walked over. The windows had all been rolled down, the loose change taken from the console. The warped, old paperback he kept in the glove box had been shredded and littered the back seat. Though the interior smelled of strange bodies and foreign fragrances, if the car started, he could still get to work on time. After a mile or two, the car felt different, the seat had been moved, the steering misaligned so that the vehicle continually pulled to one side, and the radio's preset stations had all been changed to salsa or bachata.

~

That evening Valentina found Dave in the parking lot. "It could have been worse, Dave. You're lucky you have a car. When the cops finally found the Cordovas' car, you couldn't even tell it had been a Toyota. Most people never find their cars."

"Well, I'm going to check my car every night," he said. "This is why they shouldn't allow scumbags to loiter in the parking lot."

"What's loiter?"

The boys with the soccer ball were back, and Valentina wanted to play. "Come on, Dave."

Irritated, aggravated, he declined. When Dave reached his door, he found a notice had been taped there; the headline implored, "Have You Seen Me?" A kid had gone missing from the complex. A girl. Eleven years old. Red hair. Eighty-two pounds. Dave studied the photo of a cute, smiling, happy kid. He did not want to think about where that kid was now.

The cable company had said they'd start service that evening, but they lied, and Dave grew restless. He sat at the window watching the children's soccer match. Valentina sprinted after the ball, battling a boy of ten or eleven for possession. She won control, spun, and booted the ball past the goalie. The ball banged the side of a building and ricocheted back. Valentina celebrated by putting her shirttail between her teeth, exposing her midriff, pumping high her knees, and flinging her hands into the air. For a half hour Valentina passed, blocked, and shot, cheering and high-fiving her teammates. She was nothing like the lush on the hammock from that morning. When

Mariella and some younger children arrived, looking for attention, Valentina stopped play and welcomed them to the game, reminding players to go easy on the young ones.

Dave should have fallen asleep the moment his head hit the mattress, but the apartment, being so new, did not feel like home. Dispirited, Dave rose and dressed, found in a box of knickknacks a camping knife, which he clipped to his back pocket. He worried about his car; he wondered about Valentina.

The night breeze floated down from the treetops, warm and lazy. A certain mysteriousness covered the complex as he strolled around the pool, the dark water placidly swaying. As Dave crossed the parking lot to check on his car, he passed a hulking, black pickup truck propped on monster tires. The shadowy driver, aloft in his seat, radiated hostility and disdain.

Dave's car remained where he had parked it. The windows were shut, the loose change hidden from view. Thieves would find nothing of interest here. He double-checked the doors, examined the body and the tires. A few slots down, the passenger door of the black pickup slammed and a scrawny, familiar figure scampered into the shadows. The driver had not been alone. What business had transpired? As Dave reached the truck—its steel grill like sharks' teeth—the headlights blazed to life, blinding him. The engine rumbled, penetratingly, invasively. The driver revved the engine, shifted into gear, and tore out of the spot, tires chirping.

Like most nights, Melky and his boys, wearing loose shorts and white tank tops, cranked bachata and gathered around the bed of a pickup. They smoked cigarettes and swigged Modelo and half-heartedly moved to the music.

Valentina stood among them. "Hi, Dave," she said over the music and waved. "What are you doing out here?" Valentina spoke with an air of privilege, as a native of the night.

"Checking my car."

"What happened to your car, bro?" Melky asked. He was taller than the others, better-looking, their leader. He dressed himself in gold necklaces, bracelets, and rings. Tattoos tumbled down from his shoulders, crept over his back and neck. Lifelike ink portraits underscored with birth and death years covered the backs of his hands, memorials to some dear relatives, Dave assumed.

"Some scumbags screwed with my car," Dave said.

"Lucky you got your car at all. At any moment, it can disappear."

Valentina looked on. Her blush-reddened cheeks and sultry eye shadow intimated maturity, and despite the same dirty, ragged clothes, she somehow glowed. Valentina reclined against the adjacent yellow sports car, suddenly bored. "Can we talk about something else?"

"Take a walk with me, Val," Dave said.

"Another time."

Melky grinned. "This is my hour, bro."

Dave waited a beat, but Valentina stayed firm. Tonight, she was Melky's girl.

At dawn, unable to sleep, Dave wandered from his stuffy bedroom to the living room window in time to see an unsteady Valentina stumble in from the parking lot, hair messed. She bumbled to her apartment door, and in the second before she entered, her face appeared in the porch light streaked with eyeliner.

∿

Dave carried a basket of dirty clothes to the laundry room while Valentina and friends played on the pool deck, no parents in sight. Valentina chased José around the pool. Mariella, approaching from the back side, tried and failed to wrangle the sly boy. At one point the girls cornered José until he spun and hurled himself into the pool. Mariella dove in after, floundering uselessly as José reached the opposite end. Valentina skirted the deck, now-dyed-violet hair beaming in the sun. José saw her and slipped through the gate and out of view. Valentina stopped at the gate, heaving for air. A sopping wet Mariella consoled her.

The washing machine buzzed and Dave transferred his clothes to a dryer. The laundry room door burst open and José appeared. Terror in his eyes, he pitched himself under the folding table, a chlorinated puddle forming around him. "She's going to kill me," he said, gasping, eyes darting. "The slut."

"Now why would you say such a mean thing?"

José came out from under the table, his shorts dripping, goosebumps spreading over his arms and chest. "Because it's true." He bolted out of the laundry room, leaving the door open and a watery mess on the floor.

Seconds later, Valentina arrived, followed soon after by Mariella. Valentina froze when she saw Dave. "Where's that little turd?"

Mariella pointed to the wet floor. "He was here."

"Which way, Dave," Valentina demanded more than asked.

He tipped his head, and the girls bolted, Valentina's long violet hair flashing out of sight.

∽

A week later, Dave came in from the parking lot. Valentina, her hair now dyed phosphorescent blue, her clothes unchanged, emerged from behind her mother Silvia. The squat brown woman whose humongous breasts were only slightly bigger than her belly spewed cigarette smoke from the side of her mouth and scolded Valentina in rapid-fire Spanish.

Valentina caught Dave's arm and led him away, Silvia barking at their backs. "She's always telling me what to do," Valentina said.

"Isn't it a mom's job to care?"

"That bitch ain't my mom." Valentina shouted Spanish over her shoulder, silencing Silvia. "As soon as I can leave, I will," Valentina said. "Silvia's a fascist not a mother."

They strolled to Dave's door, but he barred Valentina from entering, upset that she had chosen to spend her evenings with Melky and his boys.

"Do you have any cash, Dave? Any?"

"Why don't you ask Melky for money?"

∽

The upstairs neighbors cranked Caribbean salsa and danced overhead. Dave drove a broom handle into the ceiling with no effect and headed upstairs to ask for quiet. As he exited the apartment, he saw Valentina get into a parked car. She wasn't alone.

"Hi, Val," he said. She looked tired, drowsy, stoned. The guy cuddled beside her had spiked hair, deep-brown skin, and reeked of a leathery, spicy cologne.

"This is my new friend Rafa," Valentina said from the passenger seat. Rafa, gaunt, twenty-something, propped himself on one elbow, knocked back his head, sniffed. "What's up?"

"What are you doing, Val?" Dave asked.

"The usual," Valentina said, eyelids drooping. She shifted and her T-shirt moved, exposing the dark hole of her belly button. Enticed, Rafa fingered the rim until Valentina absently shooed away his hand.

Outrage clogged Dave's throat.

Rafa raised the passenger window and turned up the music. Reluctantly, Dave left to check on his car and on the way discovered two piss-drunk slobs in a pickup truck crooning Mexican ballads, lamenting lost loves and broken hearts, howling *amor* and *corazón*. Who and what were they waiting for?

~

Dave heard shouting and peered from his living room window. Silvia had caught Valentina by her blue hair and was dragging her down the walkway. She wrestled Valentina to the ground and sat on her back, pulling her hair and jerking her head in painful directions. Silvia landed blow after blow against Valentina's back and sides, growling Spanish all the while.

Valentina kicked and squirmed but couldn't get free.

Marco bolted from the apartment across the way. In every way he resembled an angry bulldog: fierce underbite, jutting jaw, creased forehead, bowed gait. He fired a fist into the side of Silvia's head. She yelped and slumped over, moaning in the black grass. He called Silvia stupid, promised retaliation for every bruise found on Valentina's body. Marco pulled Valentina onto her feet and ordered her inside the apartment then returned for Silvia.

She sat up, started to speak, but Marco slapped her face; the crack echoed among the buildings. Marco prodded Silvia into their apartment. The door whipped shut but the pneumatic interior lights never went out.

~

When Dave opened his door, Valentina walked right in. She said she missed him, then asked for money. Valentina looked around. "Mrs. Muñez would not be happy with what you've done to her old place." She plopped on the couch and told him about her fight with Silvia. "Silvia's gone. Back to Mexico. The bitch." Valentina lifted her shirt and showed Dave the bruises she had suffered. A blood-stained bandage covered one area. Silvia had been wearing a studded ring. Valentina dropped her shirt and tucked tangerine-dyed hair behind one ear.

She told Dave that Marco had rescued her from a Mexican orphanage when she was nine. He'd claimed to be a distant, maternal cousin and even produced authentic-looking documents. He had raised Valentina, provided her food and shelter, a bed, and he had snuck her into America, saying that America offered a hope that Mexico could not. He had enrolled her in school, told her to call Silvia Mommy. In the beginning Marco had put Valentina in swimsuits and took pictures, which he sold online. "Do you think that's why I can't swim, Dave?" Sometimes, Marco had sex with her.

Dave hid his surprise; condemnation would only drive Valentina away. What could he say, anyway? Didn't he, too, feel libidinous toward Valentina? Didn't he, too, want to protect her? Wouldn't he, too, have rescued her from an orphanage—if that story were even true? The similarities annoyed him. Still, he wasn't completely like Marco. Dave would prohibit Valentina from entering the parking lot each night. He would buy her new clothes, encourage her love of soccer and her knack with children, and he'd convince her to return to school. He'd tell Melky and Rafa and any other scumbag to piss off. He would be better than Marco.

~

As Dave laced his shoes for a jog out to the parking lot to check on his car, he calculated how much he would have to spend to keep Valentina out of the parking lot for the night, for good. How much more would it cost to free her from Marco?

Something scratched and mewed at the door. Dave peeked through the windows, the peephole. Nothing. The scratching continued. With an aluminum bat in hand he answered the door. Valentina lay on the doorstep, tangerine hair draped over her face. "Please," she muttered, "please." She dragged herself inside and curled into a darkened corner. Dave bolted the door.

"What happened? Are you okay?"

Valentina, head buried, face hidden, kept muttering. "Please . . . please."

"Are you hurt? What can I do?"

Her entire body slumped as she fell unconscious. Dave fetched a sheet from the closet and swaddled the frail, sweaty body. Her pulse was strong, her breathing slow. He placed a tall glass of water within reach and kept watch at the window until daybreak. As night turned day, danger now averted, Dave stretched out on the couch and slept.

Valentina woke and nestled beside him, head on his chest, arm draped across his midsection. They kept each other warm. Then she kissed him full on the mouth, and Dave did not resist. Valentina kissed with eyes open, her lips bruised but eager, tasting of blood and orange soda. A hint of nicotine swirled in her hair, on her clothes and skin. Her kisses came in waves—firm then tender, pure then sensual. Tingles ran to Dave's tips and toes.

With one hand, Valentina opened his jeans. He waited for her to stop, for the gag to end, and it did, but only after he had convulsed twice, three times. She released him and coiled her long hair into a bun at the back of her head. He felt flush, a spent fool dressed in shadows, lying beside a golden-haloed Madonna with swollen lips.

Valentina chomped through the eggs and toast Dave had made, gulped glasses of orange juice. Only under the kitchen light did he finally see her entire face. A sooty blackness coated her cheeks, neck, and forehead. Her tangerine hair needed a hot-water cleanse; her knees were freshly scabbed. "Thanks, Dave," she said, plucking the smallest crumbs from her plate. She was missing a tooth.

"What the hell happened?"

Tears rolled as Valentina recounted how Marco had forced her into the parking lot. "Melky and his boys," she explained. "They don't like you, and they've been wanting to turn your car into a burned-out hunk of tin." A purple bruise looped halfway around Valentina's eye; a second bruise yellowed her shoulder. "I couldn't let them destroy your car." She stared into her empty plate. "And the only way I could stop them was to keep their minds and hands occupied." Valentina's cheeks glistened with tears. "Your car is safe." She cried, favoring her lower abdomen.

He helped her stand, walked her to the bathroom, gave her a towel and clean clothes from his dresser. She wouldn't go to the hospital.

Her hair still damp from the shower, Valentina hobbled to the door wearing Dave's shorts and T-shirt. As ill-fitting as his clothes were on Valentina, Dave saw hope in the new outfit.

"I can't stay any longer. I have to go before . . ."

Dave could not stop her.

～

As Dave left his apartment to check on his car, the setting sun turned clouds candied purple and pink. The daytime heat had finally diminished, and cars and trucks packed the parking lot, customers waiting for nightfall. An outdated Cutlass pulled recklessly into a spot; neither the driver nor the passenger got out. A man smoked in a battered Honda, his eyes scanning the rearview mirror. The black truck with the shark-tooth grill had returned.

Dave came in from the parking lot. Valentina sat near the hammocks, looking after a bunch of children who whooped, tumbled, and jumped. Three kids held onto the hammocks for dear life while two others swung them. Their joy and excitement postponed the inevitable night. Valentina tied the shoelaces of a five-year-old and sent him back to play. She looked better, healed, and even kicked the soccer ball a few times. Dave, unseen, did not engage with her. Nearby, Mariella sat on a cinderblock retaining wall, swinging her feet. The soccer ball soared into the air and landed behind the retaining wall on a grassy mound. Valentina fetched the ball, tossed it back to the players. She clambered off the wall with a groan, clutched the lowest part of her abdomen, and doubled over. Valentina was not healed. With Mariella's help, Valentina leaned against the wall, breathing away the pain. Her eyes searched the darkening sky, seeking, Dave thought, a light to stay the darkness. Evening had been forced upon Valentina, and though young, her body, like flimsy hope, could easily break. And some breaks were irreparable.

∽

Dave joined the crowd pressed against the pool fence, trying to figure out what had happened. Whispers spread among the onlookers: a girl, young, couldn't swim. Where were her parents? Had it been accidental, intentional, homicidal? Grief needled Dave's flesh; woe whispered into his ears: Valentina. His heart spasmed.

The cops strung up yellow tape and canvassed the crowd, asking people what they knew. Dave knew about Marco, how he had taken pictures of Valentina and sold them online, how he sent the young girl into a parking lot full of lascivious men. The cops wanted to talk to Marco.

The ambulance crew finally fished the body out of the pool; wet red hair spilled across the deck. No one attempted CPR. Dave swept tears from his eyes, looked again, looked closely. He recognized the victim's face and she was not Valentina. This girl had gone missing many days ago, her photo posted on fliers all over the complex.

If Valentina wasn't at the bottom of the pool, where was she?

∽

Dave could not sleep. He pulled on a pair of shorts and went into the parking lot to check on his car, hoping he'd encounter Valentina along the way. Few vehicles filled the lot; not even rats nosed at the dumpsters. His car was gone. He scoured the lot end to end but only found Melky lazed against the tailgate of a pickup truck, alone, tipping a bottle to his mouth. Dave advanced from the periphery, walloped Melky in the side of the head, and pulled him to the blacktop. The bottle shattered and Melky fell among the glass shards. Dave pressed the blade of his pocketknife to Melky's throat. "I want my car."

"Wasn't me, bro."

"Bullshit."

"Look around you, bro. Why do you think the lot's empty? Even my boys is gone. Val took your car." Melky was right about the parking lot: no one smoked or drank or crooned Mexican ballads; no one loitered, counting his cash and waiting for his turn with Valentina.

Dave pulled back, drew his knife across Melky's truck tire, and heard it hiss.

"I swear I ain't touched your car."

Dave stood, reflected a moment. "I guess she's gone."

～

Dave waited, hoping his car would appear again with Valentina behind the wheel. He asked the children with the soccer ball where Valentina had gone, but they only shrugged and played on. Mariella said she missed her friend.

Dave did not call the cops or the insurance company to report his car stolen, ensuring Valentina the best chance to get away. Instead, he broke his lease, packed his belongings into a rented truck, and wound his way out of the lot for the last time.

THE CENSOR

You wouldn't think that I'd be the kind of guy to keep people from seeing the videos they want to see. Put me in a lineup of ten and no one would choose me as the porn censor for the most popular video-sharing site on the net. It is I with the glasses, the chewed sneakers, the same black hoodie every day; I with the earrings and the beard thick enough to bury Catherine's hand almost to the wrist.

I watch about thirty-five hours of porn per week. How many hours is that per year?

The censors' office for this huge internet company is a rented space behind a strip mall in New Jersey. To see our sign, you would have to be looking for it.

My workday goes like this: I swing into the parking lot and pass the deli and liquor store. There is a discrete clinic at the end—its marquee made of soft blues and pinks on a pure white background.

Todd is always in the office first because he's the only guy with the key. He spends his whole day nervously going into and coming out of his office. He rubs his chin a lot and tugs on the end of a tie his children gave him for Father's Day. He chokes himself he pulls so hard.

Todd is an example of what I don't want to be: middle-aged, neither happily nor unhappily married, neither a good nor bad dad, a guy whose entire mind is invested in work. Todd is all tasks and responsibilities, rules and policies. He makes small issues big issues and big issues DEFCON-5-biohazard-red-lights-flashing emergencies. Offhand,

Todd can tell you how many people visit the site for how-to videos or how many new channels were created in the last week. Todd is a numbers guy.

The rest of us get a cubicle: three half walls crammed with a computer desk and chair. I can sit at the desk and reach the walls with my fingertips.

I fill my bottle at the water fountain. Sixteen ounces keep my eyes from drying out.

I consider hanging pictures around my cubicle like the others do, to give it that lived-in, homey feel. But I don't want four-by-six Catherines glaring at me while I watch a girl get done by a guy with a jackhammer coming out of his fly.

Miller escapes into the green valley tacked to his wall. He wants to forget where he is and what he does. Not me. I always want to know exactly who I am and what I'm doing.

Todd comes out of his office, running around in emergency mode, always afraid the corporate gang will show up unannounced. He watches the door and tugs on his tie.

That's how it usually goes.

~

Catherine is home. A pan of cheese lasagna bubbles in the oven. Today her hair—black with strands of cherry—is curly, corkscrew curls like tiny black boa constrictors. Catherine's hair is too thick to run a hand through. Every summer, she threatens to cut it all off.

I kiss her, playfully smack her tush, feel the firm jiggle ripple back. Her cheeks are chubby and covered by a fine and delicate fur, which you can't see unless right up close. Her lips are moist, maroon pillows.

We ask about each other's day.

After I recite the morning drive, the censoring, the evening drive, Catherine recites the wake up and shower, read a novel or memoir about abused women on drugs with eating disorders, head to class. Sometimes she cries while reading. More often, Catherine gets angry. She's been threatening to write a critical essay since we met. She'll shut a hardcover and say, "What a terrible book. Why did I waste my time?" or "Why don't people know themselves? I'm going to write something that will slap people in the face."

Catherine eases into the day while I charge ahead, trying not to think too much about my station in life and what it all means. Overthinking bogs me down. Catherine teaches in the afternoons and afterward goes to an exercise class disguised as belly dancing. She gets home before me and makes dinner and washes the dishes. Guilt surges in me, like I am not doing enough for this relationship, but I tamp it down.

We sit on the couch with our plates of steaming lasagna. She asks about my day again and I struggle to think of something I haven't said already.

"The traffic," I tell her. "We inched along for miles, almost like someone at the front of the line was trying to keep us from going home."

It feels like I've told Catherine this before.

I say, "I want to get out of here. There's got to be some place that isn't this place."

I've told Catherine this before, too. "Every place is the same," she says, flipping her palms up and down like turning pancakes in the skillet. "We could leave and have different streets and a different apartment, a different driver's license, different jobs, but the problems would follow us."

She's said this before. I've never asked what exactly she thinks our problems are. I am not sure I want to know.

I tell Catherine how good dinner is and thank her. She thanks me for taking her plate to the kitchen sink. On the walk back to the couch, I stop at the moody stereo and fight it to a station playing a Clapton ballad. The music makes it seem like we are doing more than sitting on the couch.

My eyes hurt some when I rub them, and when I close my eyes, I see my computer screen. It is a good night for a drink, but all we have is wine and the feeling fades. The question Why haven't I married Catherine? is always hanging around, the way that censoring hangs around as the only job I'll ever have.

Catherine's neck muscles are tight and my hands disappear under her constrictor curls. Clapton fades out. Catherine sinks back, rests her head against my chest. From this angle, her nose is pointed like a capital A turned on its side, and her eyes are vats of fresh oil. Is this what Catherine looked like when she was young?

When she looks up at me, I flinch. From her angle, she must be seeing an older me—my chin doubled, my teeth crooked, my nostrils like industrial vacuums.

Catherine shoots up, wincing. "Ouch. You hurt." She moves her hair to soothe her inflamed neck. "It felt good for a while, then it just hurt." She is turning and twisting and nodding her head, making sure I haven't damaged her. I apologize and think, *This is why I haven't married you.*

We meet in bed smelling of mint toothpaste.

Catherine says good night but is not ready to sleep. Her freshly moisturized hand, a sunburst-raspberries scent, slithers into my boxers. We've been together long enough to know what to do and how to do it. We think we're adventurous and spontaneous, but we are vanilla. Though she directs me, I can't seem to hit her spot. But we've already spent so much time starting, we might as well finish. It's an obligation. In the dark bedroom, I can still see my computer screen; it is a white block in an otherwise black background.

"Are you okay?" Catherine wouldn't ask unless something was wrong. If she tells me I'm tired, that means the festivities are over. When I reach between my legs to see what's not okay, the deflated latex slips off. "You're just tired," she says, and I pull up my underwear and drop the wasted baggie into the garbage can. Obligation averted. Catherine kisses me to make me feel better. We hold hands only until we retreat to our own side of the bed with our own blanket and pillow. Catherine begins snoring, a feminine snarl. When I close my eyes, really trying to fall asleep now, the white computer screen appears, as though burned into my retinas. I wonder, *Is Catherine the right one?* Haven't I been wondering that forever?

Everything resets when morning comes. I leave breakfast on the counter for Catherine. On my way out, I peek at her, sitting up in bed, hair all over the place, reading *Street Bitch: One Madwoman's Life on Skid Row.* "Bye," I call and go.

The routine is so routine I don't even know how I get to work. Todd is short-stopping and tie-tugging, telling everybody, "Meeting today. Oh-nine-thirty hours. Big news. Very important." Todd's nervousness makes me nervous and that usually ruins my lunchtime appetite.

We six are crammed in Todd's office at a table that seats four. Everyone balances a pad on the thigh of a crossed leg. The home office called and told Todd that a "very inappropriate how-to made it onto the site." Mellie and Staniella handle censoring the how-to's.

"Are you awake, Gray?" Todd yells at me. "This concerns every last one of you." I was thinking of condoms, empty and useless, trying to remember the last time I saw a condom in any of the porn videos I monitor and censor. The porn actresses must all be on the pill.

"Get with it, Gray. I don't like the bosses calling me at oh-eight-hundred." He tugs his tie. "The how-to in question was posted by someone with the username Mr874Wardom." Todd waits, taps his foot until we write down the name. "The fucker how-to'd explosives and I—and the bosses—don't need the FBI implicating us because of some fucker's how to defuse bombs." How to *defuse* bombs? The how-to-*make*-bombs videos are usually the problem. "All we need is some shithead sixteen-year-old thinking he can defuse a remotely detonated brick some other shithead sixteen-year-old left in the school cafeteria." Todd shifts his weight to the other leg, becoming an irate, grieving mother. "My son died because the video on your site led him to believe he could be a hero." Todd shifts back. "We'd all be sued out of a job then."

Maybe that wouldn't be so bad.

I go outside to escape and to attempt lunch. It should be cold today, but it's not so bad, so I sit on a low cement wall, the road traffic whooshing behind me, the liquor store and clinic in full view. Inside the liquor store, college guys push dollies loaded with cases of six-packs. One guy wearing dirty brown jeans and a loose-fitting flannel shirt exits the store for a smoke break. The smoke hovers beside him.

The clinic is active with people going in. They all keep their heads down and move quickly. The front windows are tinted black. I hadn't noticed the sticker on the door before: "Female health is our priority." Aside from the discrete blue-and-pink marquee, there are no other signs.

A taxicab squeals to a stop and two women get out. One slaps a bill into the cab driver's hand and doesn't wait for change. I wonder what flu is going around. The deli will have the newspaper, but I don't move.

Lunch is a hastily made peanut butter and jelly sandwich with too much peanut butter, not enough jelly. The imbalance annoys me, and it takes a lot of water to wash down the thick peanut butter.

The liquor store is basically empty but another two women enter the clinic; still, none come out. How bad is this illness that I don't know about? After thirty minutes, twelve women have entered the clinic while only three have left. Can I catch whatever they have? They look sick as they walk to the door, faces pale, eyes almost colorless. They walk like their backs hurt and pull their coats tightly over their shoulders. They should not be so cold.

The breeze makes my eyes water. The moisture feels good, and I don't want to go back to work.

"It'll be okay," the guy smoking outside the liquor store says. I don't know if he's talking to me or the girls entering the clinic, but I don't respond and don't look at him until he crushes his butt and heads back inside.

I hop off the cement wall and, as I'm heading back to the office, the same taxi rolls to the curb outside the clinic. I wait a few beats, but no one comes out, so I go back to work.

I begin by typing in all of the usual terms: hot girl, sexy babe, hot chick, naked teen, horny slut, teen pussy, sexy ass, virgin babe, teen porn, busty babe, sweet ass, young and horny, sexy tease, stripper. Each catches thousands of videos.

Once you've done this for a while, you know what to look for. There are a great number of porn sites that use us to attract customers. We don't do anything about that. The handbook clearly states that my job

is "to remove nudity or sexual acts otherwise deemed illegal by established government laws and / or policies of this company." If a female's
nipples show, the video gets deleted. Any private parts, the video gets
deleted. Bestiality, kiddie porn, snuff videos—automatic delete. But
there are always some gray areas. Miller and I talk about it sometimes.
It's the only thing we talk about, unless we talk about sports. Miller
does what I do only his specialty is guys, mine is girls; and we share
the heterosexual and threesome stuff. He'll say, "Gray, you don't actually see cock, but you know the guy's getting it good and painful. I
mean, you see him tied up, gagged, and those are real tears squeezed
out of the corners of his eyes. I can't feel good about leaving that
video untouched. What would you do?"

A lot of these porn dealers have figured out our delete policy. They
put the first ten seconds of girl-on-girl or amateurs stripping then
cut to a commercial about visiting their website for the full-on stuff.
There is always a fee involved. I call the videos teaser-trailers.

As the afternoon rolls into night, I have deleted 124 videos and
flagged 77 users I want to keep an eye on. There was a whole series
some genius tried to sneak in while I was at lunch called "Clarissa
Studying." I've been doing this long enough to trust my hunches.
Clarissa, if that is her real name, masturbates with a glass dildo. The
kid couldn't be more than thirteen. You know the difference between
a woman's body and a girl's body. I found seven Clarissas and deleted
them all. It used to please me more, but now I just do it automatically.

There is a rumor that super-intelligent computers will replace us
soon. Is that why Todd is always yanking his tie? Well, I don't believe
it. Proof number one: Some sneaky bastards want to post porn and
know that if they call it what it is I or Miller or one of the others will
find it and delete it. So they put regular titles on porn videos, "Janelle's
Birthday," for example.

I click on "Janelle's Birthday" but there is no cake, no candles, no
celebration. Janelle is handcuffed to a banister—heels, fishnets, thong,
pasties. No warrant for deletion yet. The guy holding the camcorder
has a knife and cuts off her thong; it slingshots to the ground like a broken rubber band. Then the guy cuts off chunks of her bleach-blonde

hair. Janelle cries for real and makeup runs down her face in black streaks. Delete. Delete! I flag the user, Dyno2106. He goes in the Skunk File. The tricky bastards go in the Skunk File. There are over two hundred skunks. Some of them are worse than Dyno2106.

When I tell Miller about Dyno2106, he says, "Remember blaster-hash1?" Blasterhash1 is the first president of skunks. He's the first guy to splice a children's cartoon to an S&M video and title it "4 the kids." No super-intelligent computer will detect that. Todd had a fit that day, called a meeting. Blasterhash1 had his entire account deleted. The order came from the home office because angry parents had phoned, threatened legal suits. I'm sure blasterhash1 is still posting videos under alternate names. Why not?

My eyes dry out. When was the last time I blinked? I drink some water. Closing my eyelids is like pulling a rusty gate over a storefront. Feels like I have sand in my eyes. Even closed, my eyes still register a white computer screen; I can't look anywhere without seeing that afterimage.

The night air feels good, makes my eyes water, only now the water stings as if my pupils have microscopic cuts and the salty moisture gets in. The clinic is dark. The liquor store is lit up, carnival-style.

~

I am awoken by a hand in my shorts. What has gotten into Catherine? She is touching, exploring, waiting for a response. I wait to see what will happen. She toys. She strokes. It begins to feel good, very good. She knows the speed and pressure. I didn't think anything would happen, but now I want it to happen. Catherine takes her hand back and rolls away. I roll after her and press myself against her. She whispers, "It's okay. You're just tired." I see my computer screen again, full of videos I aim to delete. The next thing I know the alarm clock is buzzing and I have to get out of bed to shut it off. I start breakfast, all the time devising a plan. I lower the flame under the skillet and slip naked into the bedroom. Catherine's asleep on her belly, her head buried under a pillow. I lift the blankets, lower her panties. Her buttocks clench as her head snaps up. "What are you doing, Gray?"

"You know what I'm doing," I say in a throaty whisper.

She groans. "Get off."

The eggs in the skillet are beginning to smoke and burn, and I hurry to save them. After a shower, I find Catherine sitting up in bed, arms folded, a new book about growing up in a brothel in her lap. She doesn't even notice me in the doorway, holding a plate of slightly overcooked eggs Benedict and buttered toast. When I present the plate, Catherine thanks me, but puts the plate on the bedside table.

"Not hungry?"

She swings back the blankets, pulls on sweatpants, and goes to the computer desk. She opens a blank document and begins typing. She is still typing when I leave, her breakfast untouched.

I can't marry someone like this.

～

There is a cop car outside the clinic, but I head to my desk. My eyes hurt already and I urge the weekend on. I begin with coed whores today. There are over one hundred videos posted since I left work yesterday. Many of the teaser-trailers are fine, no nudity. A coed performs fellatio in a video titled "Topless Coeds"; the quality is grainy with poor lighting. By the time I delete it, the video has been viewed eight times. Who has seen it?

Miller yells over his cubicle wall, "Look out for TurnWyldeRomp."

He spells it for me. I write it on a note and stick it to the bottom of my screen.

"He's a royal skunk."

It's lunchtime. All of the coed whores that break the rules are gone, so are the naughty sluts, horny hotties, and sweet Lolitas. My sixth sense for illicit content is buzzing. Miller catches me as I head out on break.

"Did you run across TurnWyldeRomp? I'm pretty sure it was a real snuff." Miller pauses to calculate. "That's four people in six years I've seen killed on video." He awaits my tally, but adds, "I don't even think it bothers me anymore, you know, to see someone killed. It's not like the movies. You don't fight when you're dying. You kind of go passively. Your face goes slack and you bleed all over the place."

Miller lets me go and, though the fresh air feels good, my appetite is gone. I get comfortable on the cement wall. There is a second cop car outside the clinic and a square of yellow police tape strung up around a patch of grass left of the front door. Two cops talk to every woman before they let her pass. Two other cops wearing latex gloves work inside the square of yellow tape. I force myself to eat some lunch; otherwise, I'll be grumpy all afternoon. One of the cops spots me staring and I pretend my turkey sandwich is the most interesting thing in the world. All of the stock boys are on a smoke break, though only one of them is actually smoking; they're watching the proceedings next door and gossiping.

The cops in latex gloves load a large clear plastic bag with something that looks like the infant doll used to train lifeguards in CPR, only this one has a cord attached to it. The clear plastic bag gets sealed. The cop that closes the trunk catches me watching and marches toward me.

"See anything around here?" He's wearing sunglasses that hide his eyes. The wind kicks up and my eyes threaten to tear. The cop peels off his gloves. "You work around here?"

"Yeah."

"Which place?"

"The office building in back." I point.

"What do you do?"

"Computers." My standard answer.

"Were you here yesterday evening?"

"Yeah."

"Did you see anything?"

Over the cop's shoulder, his buddies pat down two girls trying to enter the clinic. The girls are commanded to open their coats, raise their arms, and turn out their pockets, before they're allowed to pass. The cop in front of me asks to see my ID. I'm glad I left my wallet in my desk.

"I don't have ID on me."

"You didn't see anything?"

My eyes water.

"Are you all right?"

"Allergies."

When I get back to my desk, I take out my calculator and tap out some numbers and write 7,280 on a note and stick it to the screen.

Miller must have done a good job on TurnWyldeRomp because I don't run into him. I write the number two on a note and circle it. Above the number I write "Miller"; below, my initials.

∽

When I get home, the place doesn't smell like anything, least of all lasagna. Catherine's at the computer, like she hasn't moved all day.

"Did you go to work today?"

Catherine talks and types without looking at me. "Of course." Her lips move as she reads her newest sentence.

"I'll make dinner," I offer.

Catherine insists she's not hungry, swears she won't be able to do anything else until she finishes her essay. "I've written fourteen pages today," she brags.

When we meet in bed, Catherine says her essay is about anger and all the things that are wrong with the world. "And," she whispers to me in the dark, "it's about revolution, anarchy, knowing yourself."

"Is it fiction?"

She cackles, "No, silly. It's all the things I ever wanted to say and never did." Her voice becomes as dark as the room. "Don't you know I've been afraid most of my life? This essay is my battle cry. I won't be afraid anymore."

In seconds, Catherine's asleep and snoring. She's too young for a midlife crisis. When I wake, she's already at the computer. An ugly energy comes from her and I hurry out of the house.

∽

Miller looks with satisfaction at the note I left him. "Only two, huh, Gray?"

"You've seen fakes," I tell him.

"No way, Gray. No way."

"People *do* fight for their lives, even if they're not too happy about living."

He crumples the note.

"Ever seen someone choked to death?" I ask. "It's rotten. When a person's got time to think about what's happening, he'll fight."

I forgot my lunch today, so I stop at the deli. They have remodeled the interior to look like a snazzy café. A petite girl with a ponytail asks what I'll have. "Turkey and Swiss between rye. Nothing else." She makes a face, thinks everything I am and everything I do is as bland as my order. It's easy to imagine her naked through her tight jeans and tank top. The newspaper catches my eye: "Cops blame pranksters for 'baby' left at clinic." The turkey sandwich is as big as a Frisbee. I eat on the cement wall and read from the local section. Every day now, cops are outside the clinic, mostly talking amongst themselves. The stock boys from the liquor store do the same. Occasionally, laughter bubbles up from one of the groups. Occasionally, someone gets shoved.

As soon as I return to my desk, my eyes begin stinging. I rub them. I close them. I drink water. I don't want to look at the screen anymore. Horny lesbians are French-kissing. That's not against our delete policy. I turn off the screen but its afterimage remains. When I touch my eyes, they tear. It takes delicate work to shut down my entire computer. The system alerts Todd.

"Did something happen, Gray?" Todd sounds like he's in my head. When I tell him it's my eyes, he says, "Get a drink of water." Todd can't manage things that are not in his plan. "Well, you've got to get back to work. You've got to."

I escape to the bathroom. When I return, my computer is on, ready for me. Before Todd can say anything, I tell him I'm getting back to work. He tries to talk anyway.

"I said I am working, Todd. Go away!"

He goes, but slowly, and I finish out the day at half speed.

Todd catches me on the way out. "Why don't you see an eye doctor?"

I hate that Todd and I are thinking the same thing.

～

I no longer expect to find Catherine anywhere but at the computer, typing furiously. She yells, "Dinner's in the fridge." She doesn't realize I am standing behind her.

I check the fridge. She ordered a pizza that looks like cheesy cardboard. I take a slice and eat it anyway. A bottle of wine stands beside the sink. I wish we had something harder. I kick off my shoes without untying them and sink into the old couch. I try not to blink because I don't want to see my computer screen and be reminded of work.

Catherine comes out of the other room, exhausted, hands on her hips, hair a tangle on her head. "I'm done," she says; the words clink to the floor in front of her, and for a second my skin feels hot and cold at the same time. She's talking about her critical essay, and asks me to join her in the kitchen for a celebratory toast. She fills two flutes halfway, hands me one, and says, "Toast me, please."

We raise our glasses, but I don't know what to say.

"Say, 'Congratulations.'"

"To personal revolutions," I say.

We drink. Catherine's lips come away bleeding red.

"To the death of fear and knowing who you are."

She pours a second glass, then a third. Catherine says she will read her essay to me, says she expects the university to reject the manuscript, but that doesn't matter because she knows an underground journal that is just crazy enough to recognize genius.

In seconds, we are on the bed. Catherine left her laptop on and its blue-white screen casts a wintry glow. The room is frozen, sheeted in blue ice. She is on top of me and I am naked. Her face burns through the frosty dark. She tries and I try, but nothing happens. She rolls off of me, onto her back, working her fingers. She grunts then melts, her fingertips moist.

A moment of recovery passes before Catherine is up and at the computer desk. My eyes won't stop tearing, tripling Catherine's nakedness. She reads her essay draft as though to a full amphitheater.

∿

At times I see the note on which I wrote 7,280 and stare through it until the numbers move and double.

Miller returns from the bathroom and leaves a wad of toilet paper by my elbow. "Keep your problems at home, will you?" he says and continues back to his cubicle. My eyes have been tearing all morning. Miller's hushed voice creeps over the cubicle wall. "You've lost it, man. You've lost it."

According to Catherine's critical essay on revolution, I haven't lost anything. Whatever it is, is snatched away from us by force, and the only way to get it back is greater force.

It's not quite lunchtime yet, but I get up, take my wallet with me, and go outside. The stock boys acknowledge me with a collective look. Beyond them, a cop, thumbs hooked into his belt, guards the clinic entrance.

One of the stock boys disagrees with the group consensus. "It was not a noose but the umbilical cord used as a noose. They used six feet of raw sausage links to do it." The stock boys jostle each other.

The liquor store is freezing inside and its halogen lights sting. I take vodka and a two-liter bottle of soda to the register. Outside again, I pour into the grass a third of perfectly good soda and refill it with vodka as the cop and the stock boys watch. The blend is perfect. The cop tilts toward me, dying to say something.

As I head back to the office, I say to the stock boys, "The sausage links probably came from the deli." They hadn't thought of that before but now run with it; their hooting sounds like chimps.

The rest of the day disappears.

∿

Today, a new cop sits in his car, window down, talking on his cell phone. A young girl with long blonde hair and big eyes, and wrapped in an oversized sweater, enters the clinic, swallowed by the tinted plate glass. She's only inside for ten minutes. On her way out, she steps around the spot where the fake hanged baby was found and goes into the liquor store.

The girl, her hood is up now, exits empty-handed. With only the slightest hesitation, she walks straight to me. I pretend I don't see her coming.

"If I give you the money, will you buy for me?" The girl pushes a fold of bills at me. "Will you?"

"What do you want?"

"Something to make me forget." She's serious.

"Oh, then you want some Irish whiskey."

She doesn't laugh.

"I'll meet you around the corner," I instruct her.

I hold the bottle by its neck; the brown paper bag crackles. She reaches for it.

"Be cool," I tell her as the cop car rolls silently around the corner. "You don't touch this bag as long as he's around."

So we talk. She says her name is Leelee, though I don't believe it. It turns out that she goes to Millwood, my old high school.

"Do the potheads still smoke in the rear parking lot?"

Leelee says that there are cameras everywhere, so nobody does shit. She notices my ring. "Do you like being married?"

The ring is from my grandfather, a silver keepsake that I have worn on my right ring finger since I was twenty.

"Sure, I like being married," I lie.

"I thought I would get married." Leelee looks at the paper bag in my hand. "When someone says he'll marry you, you want to believe it." Leelee looks at the cop, still rolling around the parking lot. "I'll probably never get married."

"I have to go back to work," I say. We can no longer wait for the cop to go away. "I'm out at five. I can meet you after."

Leelee agrees, but when I leave work she's not there.

The bottle rides shotgun as I drive home.

~

Catherine is in bed. She tells me that *she* is my dinner. "Have you been reading my mind?" Catherine says when she sees the bottle in my hand.

I remember a video of a slutty vixen who used an empty longneck bottle as a dildo. The slutty vixen had had her monthly bill too and, as she thrust, trickles of blood collected in the bottle. Work won't stay out of my mind. Is this what Todd is like at home?

Catherine doesn't let me drink myself useless, but I am useless anyway. She stops and asks, "What could possibly be bothering you?"

I don't tell her that everything is bothering me, that I want to redo life. Silence is easier.

~

The next week Miller says the job has changed him. "I'm not who I was," he explains, "but I've learned to get by."

"What does that mean?"

"You know what I mean." Miller mopes the rest of the day.

This job has changed me too, I conclude. My eyes begin to burn and tear.

~

Catherine enters the bedroom wearing only a silk robe. Her painted toenails look bruised in the dim light. She wants to have sex; I want to go to sleep. She climbs on me and, when I close my eyes, I see my computer screen. This time the screen is filled with videos I thought I deleted: naked girls bound in leather; girls strip-teasing in their bedroom; girls performing sex acts with older men, with women, with themselves, with stuffed animals.

When I come out of my thoughts, Catherine is already asleep.

~

I don't remember Dr. Marlena being so beautiful. Her lips are a glossy peach, which match her stockings. She wears the same dangerously high heels that lipstick lesbians wear to bed. I ignore the fat, winking diamond on her left hand. The world is full of married temptresses showing skin and office sluts posing. She crosses her legs; the sound of rubbing nylon reminds me of the sexy legs videos, where women put on and peel off pantyhose. Most of those videos are permissible.

"How long have your eyes bothered you?" Dr. Marlena asks.

"A few weeks," I tell her, though it's been much longer.

Dr. Marlena is probably a nympho. She has probably had sex in every part of the office—this exam room, this chair even. I smell the air for clues.

I detect a slight and sexy accent—Slovakian, Romanian, Croatian, somewhere in Eastern Europe, for sure. She uses some instruments to look into my eyes. Her eyes are a brown like honey mixed with milk chocolate. Her perfume is potent and will catch in my shirt fibers. Our lips are six inches apart, only an ophthalmometer between us.

She bends over to write in my file. Her skirt lifts some. She's a living teaser-trailer. She gives me a tiny bottle of eyedrops. "Three times per day to start, then only before bed."

~

After removing a gang-rape fantasy video, I take the note off my monitor and crush it in my fist. I've watched way more than 7,280 hours of porn. Seven thousand two hundred eighty and counting.

My eyes begin burning. I hold each eye open and squeeze out medicated drops. The solution makes my eyes burn even more. I know exactly what Todd's going to say, and I don't want to hear it.

"Then get back to work," he says.

"I am, Todd," I say but run outside with my eyes on fire.

The cops are gone from the clinic, so is the yellow police tape. Pairs of girls hurry into and out of the clinic, trying not to look at anyone. I look for Leelee to appear, demanding her money or her bottle, but never see Leelee again.

~

Catherine's breath smells like rosé, her lips taste of it. She says she wants to talk and makes me sit even before I can take off my jacket. She slides some eight-by-ten color glossies toward me. Catherine is concerned about her author photo, the one that will run alongside her essay. "It's not too late to change it."

We agree that the picture doesn't really look like her—fist under chin, gazing somewhere off-camera, implying deep contemplation, intelligence, even philosophy.

Catherine leans in. "I quit my job today." She knows that such a move ends her chances at tenure, at ever working for that university again. She shows me a check from the publisher, a hefty sum for just a single, seven-thousand-word critical essay. She wants to party, to make love like we used to, and then fall asleep cuddling. She tugs my wrist, coquettishly invites me to the bedroom.

She bought a new bra and matching lace panties. The color is called midnight purple. Her breasts, cupped and squeezed, look two sizes bigger. She backs me up, pushes me onto the bed. Candles get lit; the stereo plays. Catherine undresses me from bottom to top; her warm cinnamon-roll belly jiggles some. She tells me in a rasping whisper to close my eyes. When I do, I see hundreds of sluts trying to entice their men by parading and positioning themselves.

Catherine moves fluidly onto the bed. She spills onto me. I open my stinging eyes. Catherine purrs, "Don't even peek." She crab-walks on top of me and eases her panties to the side. My eyes sizzle and tears leak out. I am not sure who this woman is.

All I hear is quick breathing. Catherine has worn herself out. She says, "I can't do this anymore." And for the first time in ages, it feels like we might be in total agreement. We are not meant for each other. Catherine has a revolution to document, and I, I open my eyes and see, flaccid in the candlelight, who I am and what I've become: deadened, benumbed, withdrawn from desire. And now my eyes won't stop tearing no matter how much I wipe them.

UNDENIABLE PROOF
OF THE BIGFOOT

GRANDPA CHARLIE SHOT A BIGFOOT the day I was born. The bigfoot survived but Mom did not. Grandpa Charlie had been telling this story all over the state for the last eleven years, and earlier this summer, he spoke at the Elks Club, the V.F.W. Post, and the Shriners Temple. Curious yet skeptical about my grandfather's obsession, I joined him, needing something to fill the void that middle school usually filled. Grandpa Charlie quickly put me to work. He—and I, his assistant—even trekked to the Lawson Volunteer Fire Company. When the county librarians invited Grandpa Charlie to kick off Myths and Legends Month, of course he accepted, and I was right there, too. Grandpa Charlie needed the help.

The kind-hearted but stodgy librarians placed two dozen folding chairs and a long table between the obsolete computers and the storytime play area. With archeological care, I covered the table with Grandpa Charlie's collection of bigfoot artifacts, evidence, and memorabilia. Soon, the chairs filled with rural folks drawn to the county seat, recognizable in their dingy denim and battered boots, camouflage ball caps and scruffy beards or goatees. The interested but shy folks loitered at the back.

Grandpa Charlie paced behind the table, his belly pushing against the buttons of a red-and-black flannel shirt tucked into his jeans. As he moved, his thumbs rode up and down the elastic straps of his black suspenders. "The world is a lot more wild and mysterious than we think." Grandpa Charlie worked from a script he had memorized long ago. Normally, he spoke with all of the authority of a forensic scientist, as if he had studied criminology (or even anthropology) at the university, which, of course, he had not. This time Grandpa Charlie strained to sound professorial. Was it the presence of thousands of books that turned his tone, or was it simply fatigue projected in the voice of a man who otherwise loved talking about the bigfoot?

Either way, before long, Grandpa Charlie would conclude, bend to the applause, and attendees would line up to purchase bigfoot T-shirts, postcards, and bumper stickers. They'd buy "rare" photos and books, DVDs packed with never-before-seen footage, and they'd ask for Grandpa Charlie's autograph. And later, I'd help him load the truck and we'd get lunch at Larry's Dogs, ice cream included.

Grandpa Charlie pointed at me. "The day Cole, here, was being born, I was hunting turkey." Grandpa Charlie's eyes drifted beyond the library's large, tinted windows to a grassy field that sloped toward the old Hocking River. He caught himself and came back to his script. "I heard a commotion that wasn't no coon or possum; this thing sounded bigger. *Much bigger*." Grandpa Charlie puffed out his chest and widened his shoulders. "The air went sour." He mimed loading a shotgun and crept forward. "I've been in war, and I know when danger is close." He lowered his voice, and the audience leaned in, eyes enlarged, expressions harrowed. Sometimes, I, too, became engrossed in the performance. "Woods have a way of teasing the mind; they turn branches into AK-47s and palm leaves into VC boonie hats."

A man with a thick goatee and construction boots caked in dried mud raised a hand. "What'd you see?" he asked eagerly.

Expecting the question, Grandpa Charlie, with all the theatrical flair he could muster, said, "I saw a *bigfoot*." The room went still a moment. "Well," Grandpa Charlie continued, "I spooked the old boy and the Remington jumped. The shot grazed its shoulder. It stumbled forward, balanced, and in a few giant strides disappeared." Grandpa Charlie took a breath. "I never set out to find a bigfoot. A bigfoot found me, and I tell you, they exist. The evidence proves it." He stretched an arm over the table of artifacts and worked methodically through the pieces, first exhibiting eight-by-ten photos of scarred tree trunks, of shadowy figures peering between evergreens, of mutilated deer. Grandpa Charlie showed off arrowheads and brass and silver shell casings and dozens of books about the mythic beasts of Western Appalachia. He had marked and dog-eared pages, even corresponded with a few of the authors. Colleagues to the cause, he called them.

"Cliff Barrett is a good friend of mine," Grandpa Charlie said, using two hands to display Barrett's book. "Back in the eighties Cliff tracked a pod of bigfoot from California to Washington, until they eluded him at the Canadian border."

A man I had not noticed before stood slowly, leaning on a wood-handle cane, a satchel resting at his feet. He bowed slightly, straightened his shirt collar. "Stories," he said, letting the word reverberate. "The bigfoot are myth, fantasy."

Grandpa Charlie remained composed. I had seen him dispatch skeptics before.

The man with the cane, it turned out, was Yurrie Welker, esteemed professor emeritus at the university. "Tell me, sir, why, in all this time, has not one strand of bigfoot hair, not one lost tooth, not one bit of DNA been recovered?" He raised his cane like a scepter. "You, sir, are peddling fakes, forgeries, and fictions. Where's the proof?"

Grandpa Charlie told the crowd about Blaze, his long-departed hound. "One night, years ago, Blaze woke me, barking hell at something in the yard. By the time I opened the door, my apple tree had been half ravaged."

"What does that prove?" Professor Welker countered. "Science deals with proof, with verifiable evidence, not speculations and inventions. Anything could have been in your yard, sir."

"Exactly," Grandpa Charlie said. "All I know is Blaze don't bark at nothing and apples don't just disappear." He paused, losing then finding his place. "I want the truth just like everyone else."

The audience grumbled. Grandpa Charlie came around the table so that nothing separated him from them. "What got Blaze in a tizzy and ate those apples? Who and what shares the planet with us? A bigfoot, I tell you, and I shot one the day Cole was born."

"Horses and bears eat apples," Professor Welker said, refusing to yield. "It's more likely that a foraging bear startled your dog and ran off with your apples. Strange thing about the mind, we believe what we want to believe even if it's wrong. People accept that a man in a monkey suit is actually some undiscovered species."

I wanted to tell the crippled professor to shut up and sit down, to stop badgering Grandpa Charlie and let him finish the presentation so we could get some hot dogs and ice cream.

"I know the difference between a bear and a bigfoot," Grandpa Charlie said. "I've been up close to a bigfoot, and, believe me, they're real." Enduring the interruption, Grandpa Charlie moved to the end of the table and, with a flourish, unveiled some of his more prized pieces. "This is a 1964 California cast of a bigfoot print." He held the white plaster mold high for all to see; the thing was nearly as long as my arm. The print could not have belonged to a bear nor a gorilla, and certainly not to a human. Awed audience members whispered among themselves. Hauntingly, Grandpa Charlie added, "The body that belongs to a foot this large—as confirmed by an anthropologist at West Virginia University—has to be over eight and a half feet and weigh at least 700 pounds. And a creature of those dimensions would be awfully powerful."

Grandpa Charlie held a second plaster cast, this a partial print, missing the heel and cracked along the instep. The cast was misshapen, with twigs and dirt caught in the plaster. "Now this one I myself pulled from right here in our own county. No bear could leave a print like this." The cast looked to me like a hollowed splotch; it could have been anything. "If this is real," Grandpa Charlie said, "and I believe it is, this bigfoot would stand ten feet tall and weigh over 800 pounds. A bigfoot like that could easily shrug off a shotgun blast and disappear into the woods. Many folks think that the bigfoot are slow, lumbering oafs that plod about using hikers' trails. Not so." Grandpa Charlie touched his chest. "The bigfoot are quick and cunning, highly intelligent, and tremendous self-healers."

Professor Yurrie Welker groaned derisively. "Fairy tales, that's all this is."

"I beg to differ." Deviating from the usual script, Grandpa Charlie snapped his fingers at me, and I fetched a photo album from the far corner of the table. The album contained a hundred pages of pictures in plastic sleeves and weighed at least ten pounds. "Give it here, Cole," Grandpa Charlie said, aiming to silence his critic.

The photos consisted of graphic depictions of half-devoured elk and cows, headless goats, blackbirds turned to feathery mush, and wild turkeys whose bones had been gnawed. Along with pictures of vertebrae and four-inch hooked claws, Grandpa Charlie kept grainy autopsy photos of a large furry beast laid out on a steel slab, its skull uncapped and squiggles of brain oozing out. "More than one has been caught and dissected by the government, but you won't hear about that on the news and you sure won't read about it in any fancy science journal."

Side conversations about government conspiracies and secret military operations erupted in the audience. Grandpa Charlie let the chatter continue awhile. Finally, he said, "Also, a connection exists between UFOs and the bigfoot. Statistically, the chance of seeing a bigfoot after seeing a UFO increases some 150 percent." He peered at Yurrie Welker. "This could explain why the bigfoot have not been captured, why we haven't found teeth or hair or DNA."

Talk about alien intervention and abduction percolated through the audience. Patrons waiting on the check-out line swiveled their heads, drawn to the rising furor. People wanted so much to believe in the bigfoot. I wanted to believe, too, but who knew for sure? Grandpa Charlie's lectures were just performance to me. I had been listening to his stories all my life; they seemed as real as not.

"This proves nothing." Professor Welker reached into his satchel and revealed his own plaster cast, one that looked every bit as authentic as Grandpa Charlie's plaster casts. "I made this with simple wood cutouts." Professor Welker showed off the cast. "You claim to have shot a bigfoot. But you, sir, a so-called expert, didn't collect blood, tissue, or hair samples. Why?"

Grandpa Charlie faltered, as if he had been struggling forever to answer this question. "My grandson was being born that day. His mother, my daughter—I had no time. She was *dying.*"

A man in overalls, a red kerchief tied around his neck, spoke up. "If one cast can be faked, so can other casts."

"It's all a bunch of phony nonsense," another man said. "You can't prove it wasn't a bear."

Grandpa Charlie made a strange face—equal parts anger and uncertainty, as if losing more than just control of the room.

Professor Welker continued his interrogation. "Do you really think a 'highly intelligent' creature would reveal itself only to you and a band of backwoods louts? You don't really believe a whole race of bigfoot is out there, do you?" Yurrie Welker, exposing tawny teeth, wheezed laughter. "How much do you make off these good people?"

"You haven't been face-to-face with a bigfoot," Grandpa Charlie said. "You've never sensed its mystery, its magic, its power. I know what I saw." But strength and surety drained from his words.

"You are perpetuating deceit, sir. Conning people. Bigfoot do not exist."

"Who . . . ? What . . . ?" Grandpa Charlie could not recall his script, could not make a rebuttal. His cheeks sagged, and he looked at me for help. Scared and unsure, I went to him. "Maybe he's right," he told me. "If I had just thought for a moment . . . but I panicked. That's the truth. I got the call that your momma was dying and I panicked. I could have gotten some undeniable proof of the bigfoot." Grandpa Charlie's gaze moved away from me. He turned frail, quivered, and in the light from the tinted windows, became a weak, old man. By the time he had reached the hospital, I had arrived but Mom was gone. All these years Grandpa Charlie relived that day, told the same stories, yet hoped for a different ending. Now, fresh loss bowed his shoulders, dulled his eyes.

Yurrie Welker, having rested his case, hobbled out of the crowd, saying, "If you want to be duped and give your money to this fraud, go ahead." The library doors opened and Professor Welker limped through them. Several equally disgruntled folks followed after.

Before anyone else could leave, I spoke. Though terrified, once I got started, I realized I knew a lot about the bigfoot—how they use odor to discourage confrontation, how they are migratory, and how they change their coat color for camouflage. I also knew all of Grandpa Charlie's bigfoot stories—how a bigfoot once hurled rocks at his truck or that time a juvenile bigfoot plundered his garbage cans. I knew about all of Grandpa Charlie's encounters with unknown creatures and his feelings of being watched in the woods, followed, even hunted—and I shared them with listeners. The stories I told, once aired, belonged as much to me as to my grandpa, and my voice grew strong, confident, even authoritative. This wasn't performance; it was testimony.

At the end of the presentation, the audience offered polite, brief applause, and my face turned hot, but that sense of strength and confidence that had been in my voice now coursed through my veins. I could do this again if I had to, if Grandpa Charlie got that faraway look in his eye and jumbled his words.

Believers made purchases and, since Grandpa Charlie could not, I squiggled my name across the merchandise and chatted with people as if I had always been so fearless. An old lady who asked me to sign a mimeographed autopsy report said, "One day soon the bigfoot will reveal themselves." A plump librarian invited me and Grandpa Charlie back next year. I accepted on Grandpa Charlie's behalf then packed the plaster casts in foam and bubble wrap and put them in the truck. I was tired from talking and thirsty and craved hot dogs and ice cream. But Grandpa Charlie forgot about his promise to take me out to lunch, and I didn't remind him. Instead, I pondered the stories I would tell about the man who shot a bigfoot the day I was born and was changed forever after.

VICTORIES

GETTING OUT OF BED WAS A VICTORY. Brushing her teeth, changing out of sweats and into jeans and a sweater, coming to work. All victories. Indira scurried inside the shelter, savored the heat that washed over her from the ceiling vents. Cold had been gnawing her fingers to nubs all winter, and spring felt no closer. Indira pulled off her knit hat, stuffed it in her coat pocket, and punched her timecard, the start of a twelve-hour shift.

"Snowing yet?" the receptionist asked.

Indira curled her lip, gave a quick head shake, and walked toward the maintenance closet. Home was a victory, and Indira couldn't wait to snuggle into bed with her cats. The thought soothed her mind.

A doctor had taught Indira about counting victories because stress and anxiety had clogged her thinking. Victories, the doc had explained, banished blues. "They can be small, almost invisible. But you have to find them. Large or small, Indira, you need victories." He was a nice man, if effeminate. He wore grandpa sweaters and neurotically adjusted his droopy eyeglasses, played relaxation music on the office sound system. Crying, the doc believed, could be a victory too. "Find them," he had instructed. "They cure the sour mind."

Indira unlocked the closet and wheeled out a bucket and mop. She shook a carton of powdered soap into the bucket and entered the shower room. Sounds echoed back from the tile. Indira sat the bucket under the spray of shower water. Steam swarmed her like spirits rising

through the floor, wrapping her legs, swirling into her nostrils, filling her with ethereal warmth. Soap foamed and bubbled around the
mop handle, and lilac and lavender filled the room. Indira walked the
mop across the floor, under dripping showerheads, around rusty drains.
Permanent stains remained permanent. She collected Brillo pads of
black hair and tongues of old soap. Sometimes she found junk-store
jewelry, a shampoo bottle cap, or loose change. She never kept what
she found—though the thought crossed her mind—but brought lost
items to the desk, logged the date and time, in case anyone claimed
them.

When Indira finished the showers, she dragged her mop and bucket
around the dividing wall to the sinks and toilets. She used glass cleaner
and paper towels on the mirrors, poured pink hand soap into the
dispensers.

She had been overlooking the most obvious victory: fifteen con-
secutive months. Her flow had always been a nuisance, the bloating,
the meandering moods and foolish impulses. She didn't miss bleeding, waking in the middle of the night when the last pad had failed
and blood had leaked straight through to the mattress. She didn't miss
cleaning the insides of her thighs, overflowing the wastebasket with
paper towels. She didn't miss any of it.

The absence was a victory.

It was a loss, too. She couldn't deny that. Hadn't the doc also instructed her to be honest, to deal in honesty? Honestly, the absence
hurt. Could something be a victory and a loss at the same time?
Weren't victories and losses always flip-flopping?

The doc and later the gyno had agreed that the absence might only
be temporary. Lost but not a loss. Traumatic events jumbled a woman's
cycle. Happened all the time, actually. Nature's way. But, given time,
her cycle might return. That was fifteen cycles ago.

Barney had corrupted Indira's cycle, stolen her time. For a decade,
he had shackled her. But would he marry her? Indira hadn't needed
a marriage license; she simply had resigned herself to a shared life.
Kids? Whatever. And while she had grown older, Barney had planned

his escape and said no to fatherhood, at thirty-five, thirty-eight, and forty-two. Barney's clock had ticked differently, more slowly. He could be fifty and change his mind. Indira could never give birth now, could never be a mother, not in the natural way, the honest way.

Barney had left her with a cold mattress but no clothes and no dough hidden in the spice jar. The world had him now and he had someone whose cycle still cycled. "You are better off," the doc had said, though Barney owned a new house in a new state with a new wife ready to nurture a million babies, while Indira rented a one-bedroom, rescued two sibling cats, and worked at the women's shelter. Victories without losses?

Impossible.

∼

The old tenants had already checked out and new tenants waited in the registration line for a shower, a meal, and a bed. Indira leaned on the wooden broom handle, watching, studying faces, postures, their clothing cobbled together from thrift stores and dumpsters. A man talked to himself, muttering obscenities at invisible people with women's names.

"I'm sorry, sir," the receptionist behind the desk said. "Only women and children." She handed him a business card with the location of the men's shelter and gave walking directions. He turned on confused legs and, on his way back into the cold, pitched the card to the floor. After final check-in, Indira would sweep away the discarded paper.

The women came alone in torn scarves and gloves and boots, layered in sweatpants over men's jeans over more sweatpants, in oversized sweaters and sweatshirts and jackets, which hid their hands and their bodies. They pressed knit caps atop whatever hair they had. Dirty faces, red with cold, drawn with deep furrows around eyes and mouths, their eyes pale pinpoints, bleached by cold sleepless nights in alleyways guarding themselves.

The security guard searched the women as they filed past. Street women, war women, beast women sometimes carried sharpened glass or screwdrivers, aluminum daggers or needles. They arrived starved and sleep deprived, eyes glazed or bewildered, hands cut by cold, dried blood frozen in the cracks of split lips. They moved on raw knees, sucked swill from discarded water bottles, numbed themselves to cold and emotion. Most entered with nothing, their clothes in the closet of a house they'd never see again, a car abandoned on the driveway.

The rules said three nights, then you had to go. You could re-register after twenty-four hours had passed, space permitting. Three meals per day, all the canned corn, carrots, beets, and instant mashed potatoes you could eat. Sometimes hamburger meat, sometimes Spam. A cot, the showers, a dayroom to talk or play cards or board games or watch TV. A tiny bit of warmth and security. Twice per month a psych counselor offered sessions and diligently completed forms that rotted in a dusty file.

The line out the door disappeared. Dozens of women had already been admitted and congregated in the cafeteria, plunging plastic spoons into bowls of soupy, steaming gruel. One woman hustled to the registration line cuffing a boy by the wrist, thick hair swallowing his face, sneakers strapped to the wrong feet, hands covered with oven mitts, a jacket stained by motor oil, fry grease, or old blood.

She tugged and jerked him, giving dog commands to stay and obey. He whimpered about being hot, and his mother pulled off the mittens and jacket. "Stop your complaining." The boy brushed hair out of his eyes.

The pair stepped to the counter and the receptionist asked the same questions she asked everyone and put the answers on a form. The woman called herself Bibi. "Just a bit of bad luck," she said, forcing a chuckle. "We just need a few days." She leaned far forward over the counter, watching every mark made on the admittance form. "My boy," Bibi said. "I have Jordan here." The receptionist stretched her back to see the boy. "We're very hungry and very tired and . . ."

Bibi's anxiousness pulsed and skittered. The skin around her fingers had been chewed red. She twitched sometimes as if trapped inside herself. Was she a scammer, a troublemaker? The security guard gave Bibi a look. Later, while sweeping, Indira would spy Bibi's registration card: no home address, no phone number, no P.O. box, no last place of employment, no emergency contact, no relations of any kind.

Indira swept the foyer, shook rock salt from the mats, then passed her broom through the hallways. Some women said hello, most ignored her. She heaved trash bags into the dumpster, returned with numb hands, and headed straight for the hot cocoa in the main room, a former gymnasium. Army cots covered with wool blankets formed lines and rows. Some women snored; others lay with blankets tucked to their chins, staring at the ceiling, defrosting.

Indira poured hot water into a paper cup and shook out a packet of powdered cocoa. She singed her lips, stirred in a second packet, and sat at a folding table. Napkins swiped from a fast food restaurant stood in the center of the table. Heat from the cup radiated into Indira's palms, up to her wrists. She wished for spring. The bitter cold could be so unforgiving, and without snow, winter seemed spiteful.

Bibi entered, yanking Jordan after her. They moved among the cots, found an empty pair. Bibi shrugged off her outer coat, exposing an equally filthy undercoat. His cheeks crusted with dirt, the boy needed a shower. A long-sleeve shirt swallowed his hands.

Bibi stacked grub onto a paper plate and sat near Indira. She nearly gagged she ate so fast. Jordan, on his toes, worked a spoon into a vat of beans but hadn't the coordination to do anything but make a mess. After several attempts to serve himself, Jordan joined his mother, crying, frustrated, holding an empty plate.

"Don't," Bibi said. "Sit, and I'll feed you."

The boy struggled but finally mounted the metal folding chair, scratching at his tears. Whenever Jordan's mouth trembled to speak, Bibi hushed him. She worked food from one side of her mouth to the other, swallowed, breathed, and packed her mouth again. When she had scraped the last morsels from the plate, she collapsed back in her chair, sucked food from her teeth, and cradled her belly, eyelids half shut. She belched long and low, deflating her chest.

"Ma," the boy said, rising onto his knees now.

"Shush." Bibi never looked at the boy, just sat there semiconscious, sated, in a haze.

Jordan turned, noticing Indira for the first time. His dirty cheeks plumped, rounding his face, concealing his chin. His eyes, deep brown, contained a neglected innocence, glowing with caution and fright. He swung back to his mother, sobbed for food.

Before she left for afternoon rounds, Indira filled a plate and slid it under the boy's round face. "Go ahead." Indira presented a plastic spoon and smiled. "Sweet corn ain't bad with some toast." The boy attacked the mashed potatoes. "My name is Indira. You're Jordan, right?"

He ate fast like his mother.

~

By late afternoon, the women—warm, clean, relieved, and full—lounged on cots, slouched in chairs, snapped pages of outdated magazines, watched TV, swapped stories, played gin rummy. While on break, Indira passed the time thinking about Jordan and Bibi, inventing their origins, how and where they had lived, who they had been. When the stories turned tragic, Indira left them and took the mop into the shower room again.

Bibi barged in, pulling Jordan by the wrist, and propped him on a bench. "Sit. Stay." Bibi stepped from tattered shoes and dry dirt fell around them. She removed sweaters and shirts, a belt, two pairs of pants, mismatched socks; she peeled herself from dirty underwear. An odor wafted. Jordan dropped his chin, played one hand against the other in his lap. A filth-tan darkened Bibi's hands, elbows, neck, and knees. She posed shamelessly beside the pile of rags. Jordan would not look up.

"I need this," Bibi said and stepped over a lip of tile into the shower area, her hair a halo of wires. "How's the hot water in this place?" she called to Indira as she cranked the knob and tested the spray. Steam rose, and Bibi eased herself in: feet, legs, back. The spray flattened her halo and brown water swirled to the drain.

Indira moved around the boy, saying hello, smiling and waving quickly. "How was lunch?" she asked. The boy said nothing, only looked to where his feet dangled above the floor.

Indira gathered Bibi's smelly clothes, folded them, and placed them on the bench beside Jordan and moved Bibi's shoes under the bench. Indira mopped the dirty floor and tried to make friends with Jordan. The little he said confessed an unhappiness. She parked beside Jordan, clamping the mop handle between her knees. "Can I show you a picture?" Indira worked a photo of her cats out of a sleeve in her wallet. Jordan leaned in and Indira gave him the photo. She pointed. "That's Ike, and that's his sister, Liz."

Jordan wanted to know all about the cats: Where did they live? Did they fight? What was their favorite food? Indira answered his questions, told stories of the cats' silliness.

"Where did they come from?" Jordan asked.

"Near railroad tracks, behind an old building, and they were sad," Indira said as Bibi worked soap over her nakedness. "Now, they live with me. They sleep in my bed, and we keep each other warm." Indira pretended to shiver, wriggling her whole body; this made the boy laugh, his teeth yellow pebbles.

Jordan studied the photo between his fingers as if imagining himself with the felines. Indira left him to dream. She raked the mop back and forth, peeking at the boy and his mother. As Jordan had transported himself into the photo, Bibi seemed to transport herself to a tropical spa. She showered with her eyes shut, lathered and re-lathered her body, until her red flesh plumped and her fingertips shriveled.

Bibi cranked the knob, and the spray stopped. She shook water from her body, wrung her hair, and stepped into a towel, craning her head back and exhaling in one motion. The wet Bibi could have worked in an office or hosted a soiree, with her clean face and sharp features, and a towel turned into a white cocktail dress. "That felt good." Her smile and her eyes popped brightly. But when she dressed in the same dirty clothes, the lustrous shine that had surrounded her after the shower tarnished and her face hardened.

Jordan waited for his turn in the shower but never got one. Bibi
pulled on her shoes and led the boy out. "Say," Bibi said to Indira.
"How do people pass the night here?"

Indira didn't know how to answer.

"Oh, never mind."

As Bibi hauled Jordan out, he handed back Indira's photo.

A new trail of dirt led from the bench back to the door.

~

By the time Indira entered the hallway, no one was around. The receptionist had gone home for the night, and the security guard was
making his rounds. The shelter doors had been locked, allowing exits
but no entries. In the main room, women cozied onto their cots or
watched TV.

Tired, Indira wanted to go home. The cats would be hungry and
might hold a grudge if they didn't get dinner at the usual time. She
had to make the late bus.

Indira hurried to the custodial closet. She hoped to see Jordan
again, to wish him a good night, to assure him that the shelter would
be safe and that she would be back in the morning with more pictures
of her cats. The first night in a strange place could frighten a little
boy. When Indira opened the door, she found Jordan cuffed to his
mother. Bibi, her back to the door, rifled through shelves of solvents,
cleansers, and sprays. Caught, Bibi flinched, but that tough face in
dirty clothes remained steady. "Got moisturizer? My hands, they hurt
something fierce. The cold . . ." Bibi swiped some paper towels. "This'll
do. Thanks," and before Indira could speak, Bibi dragged Jordan out
of the closet and down the hallway.

The shelves had been mussed, ammonia and bleach and soap bottles turned every which way. Sometimes shelter women answered
their vices, succumbed to habit. Even mothers. Mothers should be shel-
ters for their children. Just as Indira had been when she rescued poor
Ike and Liz, had saved them from short miserable lives. Now, Indira
unhooked her coat from the nail in the door and secured the buttons,

but when she reached the lobby, rather than exit the building, she turned right. She had to see the boy, to see the peace of sleep cradle his face. Light from the open door bathed the cots in yellow dust. Women slept on their backs or sides, snoring disconsonant hymns.

Indira slipped between the rows, tracking a scent only a custodian could know. The boy lay on his side, staring at his mother. A speech worked itself into Indira's head. Someone had to speak truth to Bibi, to reorder the woman's priorities, not self first but child first. She knelt between the cots. Quick hisses sounded from the blanket Bibi had pulled over her head. Indira shook the cocooned woman. The blanket opened and out belched a chemical fume followed by a canister of bug spray, which clattered and rolled onto the wooden floor. Bibi floated in semiconsciousness; eyes lulled in liquid sockets and drool smeared one cheek, her body slack. Bibi dribbled nonsense words, her tongue fishtailing between her teeth. She sank back, eyes rolled white, arms floundered.

"Bibi," Indira said to the wasted woman. She wanted to tell Bibi about victories but didn't know how to begin. She eyed Jordan. "I am taking him," she said without anger or condemnation.

Indira told Jordan about the bus she rode to get home and the sibling cats who were probably whining for dinner at this very moment. During the talk, Bibi stirred once, gurgled, and drifted away. When Indira asked the boy to put on his shoes and his coat, Jordan moved without complaint. She helped him with his oven mitts, and the pair walked into the hallway holding hands. In the lobby, Indira stopped and knelt before Jordan. "It's going to be better. You'll see." She looked at her watch.

"Cold," Jordan said and shivered as they passed through the first set of doors.

"I know. But we'll get warm soon enough."

Indira pushed open the outer door and held it for Jordan. He stepped into the darkness ahead of her. As the door eased back, panic seized Indira. She could not get away with this. What was she thinking? The door slid on its hinge. She lunged and caught the handle with two fingertips while Jordan gripped her other hand and tugged hard toward the late bus waiting at the corner. He wanted to see the cats, to be on the bus and out of the cold.

Arms extended, Indira held the door in one hand and a wriggling Jordan in the other. The icy wind gusted around them, swirling hair about Indira's cheeks. Snowflakes fluttered like white butterflies. Her fingers were slipping, slipping. The cold brought tears to her eyes, blinding her. Finally, she let go, searching for a victory.

CLONES

WITH A LITTLE DICKERING, I got Einstein's tooth for seventy-two dollars. The doc who had taken Einstein's brain before cremation also took a tooth, and that tooth ended up in the hands of an odd-artifacts collector known only as Lance. If I hadn't been so eager, I could have gotten it for under sixty dollars.

Eggy cost me more.

Eggy wanted a *Miami Vice* yacht, a vessel with tinted glass and thick carpet and air conditioning, a 100-watt sound system, a Jacuzzi and a bar, a master suite and satellite TV, plus a motor with giddyup for jaunts to Key West. Eggy wanted an out-of-his-league woman as well, Russian, accented, young but not a girl, one with runway-model legs and super-high high heels.

Katya had to be flown over. I saved a little by going Ukrainian; Eggy would never know the difference.

After Katya escorted Eggy around town for a while, Eggy worked his magic on Einstein's tooth. Eggy was tops—or as close to tops as such illegal operations could buy—when it came to cloning. His résumé included a dozen cloned sheep, four cloned donkeys, and a nest full of cloned rats. Eggy was part of the international team that—under cloak of secrecy—cloned a chimpanzee, our closest relative, genetically speaking.

"Can they clone *people*?" I had asked Eggy.

"The practice is already perfected. But something this revolutionary takes a generation to open closed minds."

Eggy called me six weeks later and said, "Al is ready to go." We rendezvoused at the abandoned piers on the southern tip of the city, just two average cars parking at what used to be a navy ship house, then a mall, then nothing, left to rot and topple over. Not even the junkies got juiced there.

Eggy was in a good mood and that put me at ease, somewhat. If I didn't need Eggy, I'd never look twice at him. He always had a runny nose, was always sniffling, said it was allergies. I begrudgingly shook his hand. Eggy said, "Sorry I'm late. But I'm in love with Katya. She's a dream. These Russian women . . . American women are stone; Russians are amenable." Eggy had asked Katya to move in. "She's at my place all the time anyway."

Al was sitting in the passenger seat of Eggy's Subaru.

"I can see myself marrying this girl," Eggy said. He assumed I had stopped paying Katya to hang around.

Eggy promised that Al was ready to go, no waiting for an infant Einstein to grow out of diapers or finish puberty. "He was made middle-aged. Oh, you didn't think we knew how to speed up cell division? You have no idea what we're capable of. If you've seen it in a sci-fi flick, we've already done it."

I followed Eggy to his car. "Hey, Al," Eggy called. "I want you to meet someone."

Albert Einstein opened the door and climbed out, his hair a shocked splatter of gray and white, his mustache hiding his upper lip.

"It's amazing, amazing," I said.

Eggy introduced us. "Al, this is Pops. Pops, this is Albert Einstein."

He was taller than I expected, and he shook my hand like anyone else would.

Einstein said, "It's a pleasure to meet you," then, "Where are we?"

"Eggy," I said, "he doesn't sound German."

"Of course not. He's been around me and the other eggheads his whole short existence. But if you want to teach him German, it'll be cake. He has a genetic aptitude for the German language."

"Amazing, amazing."

Eggy yanked a piece of luggage from his Subaru's trunk and walked it over to my car and told Al good-bye.

Into Eggy's hand I dropped a key to a cabin in the Poconos. Eggy couldn't wait to invite Katya for a romantic weekend getaway. For an extra grand, she'd go anywhere.

Einstein was polite. He sat in the passenger seat, hands folded in his lap, seatbelt fastened, observing his surroundings: the car's interior, the crumbling pier, me. Einstein was filling that super brain of his, revving the motor. Perhaps he'd invent something before we got back to my place. Einstein was worth Eggy and the yacht and Katya and the cabin.

Wealth was one thing but renown was something else. My name was going to appear in journals like the ones Eggy reads and in history books alongside other revolutionaries.

～

Einstein ate only a few bites of the PB&J I made for him. I showed him my laptop. He didn't say a word. I turned it on, jumped on the internet, and gave him a quick tour. He didn't say a word. I showed him how to navigate, and as he started surfing, I slipped out of the room to let the genius absorb. I felt like calling the *American Journal of Physics*, the *Physical Review*, or the *Today Show*—but it was too soon.

Einstein found me in the kitchen.

"What?" I asked. "Don't you like surfing the net?"

Einstein rubbed his eyes. "Gives me a headache."

"Well, I was going to show you this later but . . ." I led him into the basement. "Your very own lab, Al." Well-lit and heated, the lab had enough space to build a long-range rocket. A large chalkboard on wheels stood along the wall. Desks and tables, pencils and notepads, spectroscopes and electromagnets waited for use. "All for you, Al, to create, to experiment, to theorize, to expound."

I showed him a stack of books I had been collecting—*A Brief History of Time*, *The Feynman Lectures in Physics (Vols. I–III)*, *The Quantum Universe*, *Quantum Theory of Optical Coherence*. His mustache ruffled in what I took to be a happy way. I started to leave, to let the genius work undisturbed.

"Where are you going?" Einstein asked.

"I want to give you peace and privacy in which to work."

Einstein looked at me curiously. "Work on what?"

"I don't know. Maybe physics. Maybe E=MC². "

"What's that?" he asked, his mustache steady.

"Don't play with me, Al. You know E=MC². "

But he didn't know, so I walked over to the board and wrote out the formula in white chalk.

"Very interesting," he said. "But what can I do with that?"

"I don't know, Al. You're the genius."

I couldn't help scolding Einstein. My investments always promised a healthy return.

Einstein tried to follow me out of the basement. "No, Al! You stay here. Read a book. Theorize, for Pete's sake!"

He gave me his best sad-boy look as I closed the door, locking him in.

I called Eggy's phone. The connection was spotty.

"Can you hear me, Eggy?" I wanted to make sure there was no confusion because I aimed to castigate him. His voice cut in and out.

"Es, I can ear you."

"You made me an Einstein that doesn't know jack-squat about physics or relativity or energy. What the hell!"

"You wanted Stein; I ot you an exact genetic copy of the an."

"He's worthless!"

"You can each him. Et im some books or something. He has a genetic aptitude for math and science."

I stopped myself from threatening Eggy's life because Al Green was playing in the background. "Where are you, Eggy?"

"Poconos. With Katya. I'll be in the lab on Monday. We'll alk then. I have a surprise for you."

Before I could say I hated surprises, the cell signal vanished. I couldn't get Eggy back on the line. I wanted to string up that mad scientist and quarter him, make him suffer, take Katya and all his other toys away.

Einstein tapped on the basement door, asked to be fed. I told him to work. He begged for a glass of water at least.

"Show me a new theory, Al, and I'll give you all the water you can drink."

～

The navy ship house looked the same as always, abandoned, a blight along the river, a sore left to fester.

When Eggy got out of his car, I strangled him. I berated him about Einstein, said I should take back the yacht, the cabin, and send Katya back to Ukraine. His face turned red in my gloved hands, yet he managed one word that saved his life: "King."

I eased up. "What?"

He needed a moment to breathe again. "Did you say, 'Ukraine'?"

"Focus, Eggy. Who's the dark-haired guy in your car?"

Eggy whistled to his passenger, and Elvis Presley strode to us, guitar in hand. He was dressed in jeans and cowboy boots, a white undershirt. This was the young and fit Elvis, the pre-drugs, hound dog, rock and roller. His lip lifted. "Howdy, partner," he said to me and snapped and pointed.

Eggy said, "You know, the thing about science is it's always improving on itself. We are always tinkering."

"Does Elvis play guitar?" I felt like I was about to buy shoddy stocks.

"Show him, King."

Elvis slung the acoustic over his freshly greased coif and set his hips. As his guitar pick hovered, ready for a massive downstroke, my heart crammed my throat: This is The King! Elvis ripped through "Jailhouse Rock" and "Blue Suede Shoes." I couldn't believe what I was hearing, definitely not some imitator.

Eggy said, "It took a little tweaking of the gene sequence, but The King has the entire Elvis catalog memorized." Eggy reflected. "Isn't this a great partnership we have? You give me treats and I give you treats. Elvis is going to make you rich."

"I'm already rich." But I wanted more.

～

The woman at Sony Records, Candy Coulé was her name, broke out in red hives when she saw The King in her office. "I've seen some impersonators, let me tell you. I lived in Vegas for six years, so I know a good Elvis when I see one." She asked The King who his surgeon was, where he bought that nose, who gave him those lips.

Elvis idly plucked a guitar string.

"He knows all the songs," I told her, "and he sounds even better than the digitally remastered collection."

When I winked at The King, he strapped on the guitar, swiveled his hips, and lifted that lip. The guitar pick paused dramatically and fired. The King—such a showman—seduced Candy with "Love Me Tender" and leveled her with "Can't Help Falling in Love." She slouched in her leather desk chair like a wet towel. Her brow glistened. "Simply awesome," she managed. "If I wasn't happily remarried . . ."

I stepped between Candy and The King. "As his manager," I said, "we are prepared to give Sony first, exclusive negotiating rights. We want to be part of the Sony family." I invited her to make an opening offer.

"Huh? What?" Candy Coulé came out of her lullaby. "What are we negotiating?"

"We're prepared to sign a contract today," I assured her.

Candy sat up, her features hardened. "He sings great, plays great, and my goodness does he look great, but on the Strip, he's a dime a dozen. Granted, not many play the young Elvis but . . ."

But this is the real Elvis, I nearly blurted.

"We've heard these songs before," Candy said. "We've seen this act before, and we've already bought every reissued album. Now, if you can give me something new . . ."

"New? This is The King! Songs swim in his blood. Play her one, partner."

Elvis started to play "All Shook Up."

"Play something new," I said, and Elvis looked at me, jerked his head so that a curl of hair fell between his eyebrows. I pulled him aside.

"Play a song we haven't heard. Something new."

He eyed the fretboard, urged his hand to make a move. "I don't know any songs that aren't songs I already know."

"What? Can't you wing it? Can't you write something right now? What about the songs swimming in your blood?"

"Maybe they're in my blood, but they sure ain't swimming."

I was already planning Eggy's sudden disappearance.

∽

On the ride back to the airport, I let Elvis have it: "You embarrassed yourself, me, us. You're Elvis frickin' Presley, and you can't come up with one of your own songs! Candy loved you. We could have a deal right now. We could be famous!"

The King said that the real Elvis didn't write many of those songs we think of as his.

"Shut up, King! You *are* the real Elvis."

At the stopover in Dallas, I headed to Applebee's for a quick meal. The King said he wasn't hungry. After I finished and paid, I couldn't find The King anywhere, so I flagged down an airport security guard.

"What's your friend look like?" the guard asked.

"I told you. He looks like the young Elvis, pre-sequin jumpsuit, carrying a guitar."

The guard radioed the description, adding, "No, this is not a joke; no, this is not a drill."

An hour later, the guard, with a smirk he couldn't hide, told me a guy fitting The King's description boarded a bus headed toward Memphis. I had to run to catch my own flight and let The King go.

∽

When I got home, finally, all I wanted to do was shower and change, lay in bed with a bowl of cookie dough ice cream and watch *Cops*, only the ice cream was gone and a stupid reality show about tattoos was on. After a ten-and-a-half-hour nap, I rose and wandered the house, trying to decide how to repair my frayed life and get famous. I realized I'd been hurting myself by keeping my cloning operation a secret. Why *couldn't* I include the media? The hype would make people pay attention and curiosity would get them to stay tuned in. But first I called Lance to see if he had any more teeth for sale.

Elvis had been a mistake. I had let personal glory cloud my judgment; I had let the idea of a thousand screaming girls with wads of cash in hand influence me. Even if Elvis could write his own songs, there was no guarantee he could make it big in the current music scene—not with Auto-Tune and a million American Idols, and bands that don't know how to play any instruments. The music industry was too slick, too phony.

And Einstein was a mistake because—Einstein! I forgot that I had locked him in the basement four days ago.

The door was still locked solid and a peculiar odor wafted from behind it. A white fold of paper sat in the slit beneath the door. I unfolded it and stood.

"Dear sir," Einstein wrote. "I do not deserve to be treated like this. I am a human being and I have rights. Please, let me go free. I have begun reading the first of the books you locked me in here with. Quantum physics is a topic that interests me, but every time I read, my eyes get heavy. I can't read more than a page without snoozing. Besides that, I'm so hungry! and thirsty! that I can't concentrate long enough to absorb the information. If I were better versed in chemistry, I'd make an acid with which I could erode the door lock and free myself. Or I'd grow yeast and make some food to sustain myself. As it is, I fear I have lived my last day, seen my last sunset. Though I am religious in name alone, I pray for kindness and compassion to enter your heart, for you to liberate me from this personal death camp."

Einstein signed his letter with "most sincere respect."

I held my breath when I opened the door and peeked long enough to see a pale, corroding hand and fingernail scratches in the wood of the door.

∽

Eggy called me for two reasons: he got the tooth I sent him, and he proposed to Katya at the Poconos cabin. She didn't say no. This was

Eggy's last chance. I had heard about a Chinese dissident and defector who could makes clones at half the cost.

Some weeks later, Eggy and I met again at the pier. Two people sat in his car.

"I have someone I'd like you to meet. I think you'll be very pleased. She turned out better than I could have hoped. It's all in the genes," Eggy joked.

Katya reluctantly got out of the car and strode like a runway model to us. Her long legs poured out of a short skirt. She wore sky-high heels and metallic eye shadow, her hair teased. Katya was flat-out hot, but not gorgeous. Up close, she looked used.

"Tell him the news," Eggy said to Katya.

"That guy in there," she pointed at the car, "is a sweetheart."

"No. The news about us." Eggy grabbed Katya's hand to hold.

Katya wiggled the chunky diamond on her finger. "We're married!"

Eggy said, "Best move I ever made. I can't wait until we start having babies!"

"Congratulations," I said, not meaning it. "But where's my guy?"

Eggy called out, "Hey, Johnny!"

A man in a suit, hair parted to the side, stepped out of the Subaru. Eggy introduced me to John F. Kennedy and we shook hands. His eyes stuck to Katya.

"Does he know who he is?" I asked Eggy. "Does he know the history?"

"He knows everything. A tweak of some key brain-memory cells was all it took. We also filled him with the history since 1963." Eggy made a finger-gun and pointed it at his skull.

I handed over two first-class tickets to Hawaii.

Katya took the tickets. "I've never been to Hawaii!" She gave a quick wink to JFK and headed back to the car.

Eggy followed her but called back to me, "Where are Al and The King?"

Was he trying to upset me? I gave him a wife and a Hawaiian vacation. He gave me duds. "They . . ." I began, not knowing what to say. "They are in a better place."

Eggy waved at me. "I'll send you a postcard from Maui."

When I looked at JFK, he had a hand on his chin. He straightened. "They seem like good people. Katya's a darling."

I told JFK to get in the car. He looked like President Kennedy, talked and gestured like him, had the same charisma and political outlooks and ambitions. He wanted to change the world as we knew it. I sent a release to the media.

∿

When the calls started and news reporters showed up at the house, they asked the same question and I gave the same answer. "No, he is not the former president brought back to life. He is not some clone manufactured in some lab. That's unethical and illegal. His name is John Francis Kennedy." I told the media JFK would run for president because he believed America could regain its place as the greatest nation on Earth. The career politicians had been mucking around in our nation's capital for too long. JFK played well on TV; the ladies of *The View* loved him, Oprah, too. He appeared on *Good Morning, America* with expensive chocolates for the hosts. Letterman thought JFK was the coolest. The *Times* and the *Washington Post* endorsed JFK and the primary was a cinch. Each evening, JFK excused himself and retired to the study. There, behind the closed door, he sipped malted Scotch and read book after book about his genetic twin, John Fitzgerald Kennedy.

One night I joined him in the study for a drink and JFK thanked me. "Someday, I'd like very much to return the favor."

"What do you mean?"

"If you die, I'd like to clone you."

"Hush! Don't say the C-word. You never know who could be listening. And who's talking about death anyway?"

JFK was already returning the favor. As his campaign manager, my name was in the news as much as his and, after victory, he'd likely put me in his cabinet, though I wouldn't object to being named ambassador to the Bahamas.

JFK leaned forward in his chair, slid his tumbler onto the table, and said, "I don't think Oswald acted alone."

"What?" My tongue went limp in my mouth.

"I don't have any proof, just a feeling, a hunch in every nucleus of every cell in me, as if my genes know."

By the time I got Eggy's Maui postcard, he was back at the Poconos cabin, enjoying married life. I didn't pay much attention to Eggy anymore; the campaign took all of my time, and it was better, politically, to distance myself from the likes of him. Pretty soon, I would be in the White House and would forget Eggy's name altogether.

JFK left the house for fundraisers and rallies, where huge, enthusiastic crowds chanted his name. In the evenings, JFK snuck away to practice his speeches. He spent hours, he said, in a rented motel room, rehearsing, trying to capture the perfect pitch, cadence, and tone to hammer home his messages of change and rebirth.

A week before the general election, with JFK more than ten points ahead in the polls, I got a call from a reporter who told me he had evidence, lurid and undeniable, of JFK and some married woman. I told him to take his piss-poor attempt at blackmail and shove it.

When JFK returned from speech practice at the motel, I asked him how it went. He told me he had crafted a speech that would titillate and inspire. "We're going to win this election," he promised.

I asked JFK if he was really at the motel.

"Yes."

"And were you really working on your speech?"

"Yes."

But that was not true. The truth was that JFK had been gallivanting with a married woman, several actually. I sent JFK to bed immediately and without his glass of Scotch and ordered him to keep his pants on until after the election.

The day before the election, we scheduled a rally in the city; the governor and mayor would attend along with thousands of sign-waving, T-shirt-wearing JFK supporters. It would be a great photo op. JFK walloped the crowd with a speech that could energize even the most disaffected and apathetic.

Then JFK moved through the throng, cheek-kissing and hand-shaking until Eggy blocked our path, his face red, his eyes wet.

"She left me," Eggy said, his voice cracking. "Katya's gone! Before she left, she told me she slept with JFK, and when I asked why, she said she didn't love me. And she wasn't even Russian!"

Since their honeymoon, I had stopped paying Katya to keep Eggy happy.

JFK couldn't deny the accusation, so Eggy pulled out a snub-nosed pistol and jammed it into JFK's gut. I promised Eggy I could get Katya back with one phone call. I'd simply wire her a payment and a ticket. But the gun popped and flashed, and I and everyone around us jerked back, shielding our faces. Eggy fired a second, third, fourth time before security officers tackled him to the ground. Eggy got off one more shot, a bullet to his own head.

I leaned over JFK, blood spilling from his chest and stomach. He chuckled at me. "I always wanted to do it with a Soviet," he said. "Those Ruskies have always been naughty." JFK died on the sidewalk despite my calls for him to stay awake. I had enough of his blood on me to make a clone, and some of the other eggheads in Eggy's lab expressed interest in owning a yacht, a Poconos cabin, and a Russian babe. But I was done being famous.

THE PUB RUNNER

CITY LIGHTS FRAGMENT THE DARK as a dozen of us crowd the sidewalk wearing shorts, a number pinned to our cotton T-shirts. Some of us stave off the cold by bouncing in place or stretching hamstrings one last time. An official marks the starting line, keeping runners back with a hockey stick held horizontally, his face blue from the light of his smartphone. Runs always begin with such seriousness, the runners eager, excited, unsure. Most have never done this before.

At exactly the top of the hour, the official claps his hockey stick loudly on the cement, simulating a starter's pistol, and the race begins. Not far from Oregon Street, we charge northeast on West Passyunk. For the first quarter mile, I always want to quit. Runners pass me on both sides and will tell their buddies later that, at least for a second, they were ahead of Rick Trestle. I let the college kids go, let them make the mistake. They won't be around when I get to Walnut Street.

The middle of the pack welcomes me.

Black ink scrawls across my forearm like a tattoo gone awry, listing the stops along the route. Ooglies, four-tenths of a mile from the start, mimics a schoolhouse with its brick façade and large wooden door. The only window is stuffed with a battered A/C unit.

The race leaders hurry out, scowling at us, as we run in. Another official monitors from inside Ooglies, hands on his hips, ready to call an infraction. Mugs of foaming amber wait for us middle-packers. While some gulp and some sip, I hold my breath and guzzle, a tactic to minimize air bubbles and burping. Bloating is dangerous for a pub runner.

We down our brews (confirmed by the official) and sprint to the exit. Jacked ankles and tweaked knees happen most often when runners enter or exit a pub, but we middle-packers are fine. I've seen runners bang blindly through pub doors, miss the steps, and crash on the beer-dampened floor. Some only tear ligaments, others break jaws and crack teeth.

The night feels warmer now, and I'm beginning to sweat. Already, a few of the slow pokes have quit running and shuffle along far behind. They'll never get to the second stop.

~

Leanne, of the sparkling brown eyes and raggy spiked hair, talked a lot. She would pause only to touch a finger to her lip and say, "Um . . ." before her mouth reloaded and a new round of words flowed forth. She soliloquized and I listened.

Leanne protected herself by blabbering, as I protected myself by listening. But, together, we took a chance. Leanne listened and I spoke: "Want to go out?"

"Yes," she said immediately. "Yes!"

~

Squires Pub and Meeting House, a white-walled square on the corner of Thirteenth and Morre, claims to have been established in 1776. The slogan on their napkins reads: *Serving patriots since day one!* A standing cinderblock acts as doorstop, and we middle-packers stampede into a boiling box. The official greets us: "Just try and cheat, you bastards." He's drunk.

All the men of Squires wear ball caps and week-old scruff and hover protectively over their mugs, not speaking a damn word. Johnny Winter's "Be Careful with a Fool" wails in the background, his Gibson a-bellyachin' and a-ramblin'. The TVs broadcast the last innings of another Phillies debacle.

When I first crossed the Delaware and took up residence here, not knowing one block from the next, one person from the next, I frequented Squires for its quiet depression, its blues, and its chicken fingers. I enjoyed listening to drunks commiserate, thought it fun to try to follow their beer-warped logic.

The other runners and I hoist full mugs to our lips, the official glaring, his whistle plugging the corner of his mouth. The beer at Squires tastes like it was brewed in 1776 and left in a warm room for two centuries. A skinny, young runner tiptoes out of a beer puddle, shaking droplets from his brand-new sneakers. He won't last. Most runners don't have the disposition for discomfort, for a distressed digestive system, for a swirling head and a pounding heart, for a belly full of booze and a palpable, insidious nausea. They don't care about winning or finishing, really. Their mission is fun and severe intoxication, even blackout; the run is just a coincidence.

I hustle back into the night, warm suds sloshing around inside. The intersection of Passyunk and Carpenter buzzes with traffic. Until now, runners could just zip across streets with only a glance in either direction. Carpenter is all about timing, finding gaps between the flow of cars, so you don't break stride. All the while, cabbies actively hunt pub runners: horns blare, fists shake out of open windows, and the night fills with curses in Swahili, Urdu, and Igbo. Running blindly from one block to the next could cost a runner his life or limbs. The field thins as three loafers quit at the curb and turn back for another Squires brew. Soon, only the stubborn and determined will remain.

One half block ahead, the leaders' sneaker reflectors flitter like lightning bugs. After a mile, the two pints I've drunk strike my thighs. The muscles threaten to spasm; my stride shortens, my toes tense.

～

I practiced for my first race by buying a six-pack and a one-day pass to the Christian Street Y. I selected a concealed treadmill and started running. Every half mile, I paused, chugged a beer, and hopped back on.

Five beers and nearly three miles later, an attendant with a giant Y on her shirt confronted me.

"Sir," she began. "What do you have in the bag, sir?"

"Nothing." I played sober.

"I smell beer, sir." She reached for my bag.

"That's private property. You have no right!"

"I could call the police, sir," she said.

"Listen, I'm in training."

She walked away but not very far, and at the three-mile mark, I cracked another beer and chugged.

"Sir, alcoholic beverages are . . ."

I quit listening because, I noticed, my legs worked effortlessly. Somehow, I possessed an innate talent for running drunk.

The attendant reached for the emergency stop button, but I smacked her hand away. "That's dangerous," I said. She reached again and we tussled. My foot caught the guardrail, and the rolling belt threw me. The empty beer cans spilled out of the bag, clattering like pathetic sleigh bells. The attendant accosted me, stood me up, and told me to get out. I responded by puking all over her Y shirt.

～

Most of the pub runners are natural drinkers. They can guzzle gallons and stay upright, walk straight lines, touch their noses with their eyes closed, balance on one foot, solve quadratic equations, and operate motorized vehicles. They don't puke and they don't pass out. But they don't run either. They think a few laps in Rittenhouse Square will make them runners. Not so. Running is hard on the soles, the ankles, the shins, the knees, the quads, the hip joints, the back. Alcohol tolerance isn't enough, pub runners need a Kenyan's heart and a cheetah's lungs. It's better to be a runner who learns to drink than a drinker who attempts to run. Most of all, pub runners need a mental escape.

～

After Leanne and I moved in, I would run home, excited to find her reclining on the couch, watching reruns, her smooth stomach peeking out of her tank top, hair on end, her scent filling the place. She'd wear my boxer shorts, those long legs inviting, those tiny blue toes winking. We couldn't stay away from each other. Leanne would catch me watching her and attack me. We'd practically dehydrate ourselves. I'd pull and she'd pinch; I'd nibble and she'd tug.

∼

The Keg 'n Barrel's sign uses gilded Old English lettering on a black background. Inside, the stained-wood booths appear sturdy but lack cushions. On one wall a Union Jack glows under a spotlight. The brass taps gleam with regal affluence and are topped with uniquely carved handles: a Bass bowling pin, a Fuller's shield, a Newcastle Brown arrow, and an unmistakeable Guinness pint.

Four race leaders are raising their mugs when I jog over. They glower because I have caught up to them. One leader, Trevor, has a red nose and cheeks, his shirt sweat-glued to his body. Trevor shoves past me, grumbling something that sounds like a black-magic spell for my legs to go limp. Whatever. Intimidation doesn't work. My thighs have dismissed any sluggishness, my feet crave pavement, and my gut has quelled revolt. And mentally, I'm not even here. Mentally, I'm on the couch with Leanne, frolicking.

I hold my breath, guzzle, and plunk down the mug. My vision blurs only when I quick-turn my head or eyes.

I bank right out of the door. Monroe inclines deceptively, slowly. Runners wonder why their knees whine, why their hearts hurt, why I have just caught and passed them. At the top of the slope a runner stumbles, crumbling into the shadows, landing facedown at the base of a building. As I approach, Trevor's groaning like a whiskey-laden bum, a soupy halo of puke surrounding his head. He opens his eyes just enough to see me pass and hisses, "Fuck you. I hope you lose."

Ahead, the Monroe and Fourth Street traffic light beams red, so I downshift, slowing, waiting. When it turns green, I fly. The leaders are not far ahead now.

I join the lead pack, and we pit-stop at bars four, five, and six. These runners have developed a tolerance for alcohol. At this stage, six pints and more than two miles down, runners welcome beer's numbing properties. If their feet blister, they can't tell. If their calves seize, they don't notice. Some of them puke on purpose, to purge the alcohol. There's no rule against it.

Confusion is a bigger problem than numbness. A wrong turn, the wrong bar, can end a runner's chances. Other runners make the worse mistake of overthinking, rationalizing: Why did I believe pounding beer and running would be fun? Why run when I can jog? Why jog when I can walk? Why leave the bar when I can just stay? Who cares about a trophy and trivial glory?

I'm drunk now but not so bad that I can't hear Leanne giggling as I plant kisses on her belly.

~

Leanne fell in love with me first. She showed love in little ways: a hand-hold, a quick kiss, an admiring glance. Leanne and I slept, shopped, ate, and watched movies together. We didn't get bored or anxious or claustrophobic. We thrived.

We joined the first pub run together. Our goal was to finish, not win. Leanne had worn black tights with pink lightning bolts down each leg and a sports bra that packaged her boobs nicely. Pink sneakers and tiny white ankle socks completed the ensemble. I dreamed that she was the race I was trying to finish.

Within half a mile, Leanne wanted to quit. She'd been complaining since the first block about fatigue and knee pain. One swig into her second beer, she choked and coughed. "I hate beer," she said. "Tastes like goat piss."

While on our way to the third pub—Leanne floundering badly—I slipped in behind her, shouting, "Let's go, Leanne. Come on."

Her neck and back were sweat-shiny, her spiky hair wilting. "I don't feel good."

"You can do it."

She told me to shut up.

"But our goal," I said.

That quieted her.

Just before the next stop, Leanne, in mid-stride, sprayed puke all over the sidewalk, her sneakers and tights, her sports bra. Vomit—reeking of hops and barley—misted back into my face. Her hair and nostrils dripped beige slime. I offered my shirttail, but she slapped it away. "Don't touch. Get off!" Leanne kept saying. "I'm done. This is stupid, Rick. I mean, who willingly does this kind of thing?"

The next pub stop, Cobb's, stood a stride away. We were so far behind the other runners that the official had already put his whistle away. "You must be bringing up the rear," he slurred.

I drained my mug, but Leanne sipped and dribbled, and beer ran over her lips, down her chin, mixing with the vomit.

She put her mug next to mine.

"What's that?" the official said, peering. "Gotta finish the whole thing."

"It's close enough," Leanne said, wavering on her feet.

"Just a few more gulps," I said to Leanne. "You can do it."

She stared at the mug a long time, stifling burps, then said, "No. I can't, not a bit more." Leanne turned away from the mug.

"You're disqualified," the official said and recorded Leanne's number on a card he'd removed from his shirt pocket. "Your race is done, sugar."

Outside, Leanne apologized to me. "You should keep going," she said. "I'll meet you at the finish." I took off running, chasing the end. Meanwhile, Leanne pursued her own finish line.

From that day, Leanne hid behind headaches and sleepiness and menstruation and work and exhaustion. First, her kisses lacked power, then they gradually ended altogether. She no longer wanted to watch movies together or food shop or stroll through the park. We ate meals separately and cordoned ourselves at opposing ends of the apartment. I would goad her sometimes to get a reaction—clenched fists, stomped feet, a bared-teeth growl: "You're infuriating!" Soon, she quit reacting altogether. Nothing I said or did bothered her. She was neither kind nor unkind, neither civil nor uncivil, yet something seethed inside. Leanne settled into a nonplussed, apathetic version of herself. And I mimicked her withdrawal.

Despite this, she didn't leave.

~

After Spruce comes Eighteenth Street then a diagonal sprint across Rittenhouse Square. The finish line sits two blocks up Walnut. But before that is Cannon's Taproom.

I catch the heels of a pale-armed waif with the number fourteen pinned to his old Masterman High X-Country shirt. He's hardly sweating, hardly exhaling, and can't be more than a week over legal. He'd fit right in at Penn Law with those crisp brown locks and that economical gait. He probably wears a fit tracker and carries a photo of Larry Page in his wallet. In a straight race, this Road Runner would destroy me—that lean frame, those monolithic calves. But this is pub running.

I pull stride for stride with him. We burst through Cannon's door at exactly the same time, hoist mugs, and drink. He may be fast on his feet, but I'll pull ahead in one gulp and get out first. I'll win by a mug.

I knock back my beer in record time and give the Road Runner a sarcastic "So long, pal!" but he's done too, and as we charge outside, other runners wobble in, sallow-faced, puke-stained. They stink.

The Road Runner and I bolt across Eighteenth and enter Rittenhouse Square, matching step for step. Rather than quaver and weave, he runs steadily, appears Olympic. "Think you can't be beaten?" he says.

He tries to pass me, but I cut him off. There's no rule against it. Every time he makes a move, I block him with a shoulder, an elbow, a hip. Sometimes our legs swipe and slash each other like a quartet of dueling sabers, but he's got no hope of passing me and I can practically coast to the finish.

I whip onto Walnut and when I peek, my challenger dashes into the street. He's got no choice but to take the perilous way to get around me. No way has he got the gas for this gamble.

As we're flying past Holy Trinity, an engine roars, tires screech, and a cabbie curses. The cab cuts the Road Runner's legs out from under him. He caroms onto the hood, then rolls over the front bumper and onto the pavement. Ever determined, the kid attempts to stand but stumbles and collapses, his leg disjointed at a sickening angle. He cries himself into shock. The tug of humanity grips me, begs me to stop, to quit, but I slip away, fleeing the scene. Mentally, I'm not even here. Mentally, I'm with Leanne, trying to reconcile, trying to stop her from leaving.

To this point, Leanne has stayed because she's had nowhere to go. These last weeks, she's been saving to get her own place and purposely waited for tonight's run, when she knew I'd be gone, to make her move. I'm not supposed to know she's moving, but it's hard to hide (boxes and bubble wrap and packing tape) from a person who shares the same address.

My thighs might be burning, my fine-motor skills failing, but I wouldn't know it. I run myself into long corridors of deep contemplation. The run is a personal test, a choice, free and clear, to move, to drink, to court illness and injury, to stop. I can quit anytime I choose but don't because it's easy. Leanne thinks the best pub runners must be supreme masochists. I can't disagree.

The finish line is not actually a line; it's the Mercury Tavern, a sliver in the wall between a bodega and a laundromat. I amble in to pound the last beer and claim victory. The crowd cheers. Spots like black-and-white firecrackers fill my eyes. Sweat drips from my wrists. Spectators wave napkins, clink glasses, and hurrah. As I draw the final mug to my lips, they chant: "Chug, chug, chug!"

Two officials stand close, assessing then confirming with nods and raised arms. Not a drop gets away from me.

People take video and pictures of me hugging the trophy. "What's your secret?" they ask.

To separate yourself from the pain, I think. I tell them that Kenyan marathoners conquer distances not because they seek the finish line; their end, their glory, is somewhere farther, in a deeper consciousness, in the recesses of the heart. The Mercury erupts with loud music and dancing and shouting. Everyone knocks back shots, and in the madness I sneak away, my race unfinished.

Just outside, I bump into the Road Runner, ghostly and ruined, his leg dragging behind, his arm draped over the shoulder of the cabbie who hit him. The cabbie says, "Jeez, man. He won't go to the hospital, the fool."

"Here," I say and push my trophy at the Road Runner and scamper up the street. My finish line lies blocks ahead and time is short, so I take my chances in the street and run home as fast as I can.

THE DYING MALL

LORN OLSEN JITTERED. The quivers started inside, where tendons and ligaments joined bone. A side effect of his medication, the quivers racked his head and occasionally blurred his vision. Throughout last summer, Lorn had worn long pants because his legs shook and his knees knocked, often painfully. Sometimes, Lorn wished the slow and constant knocking in the center of his chest would stop, too. The pills were supposed to eliminate that wish.

Bugs—another side effect of the medication—moved under Lorn's skin, their spindly legs danced down his arms or marched up his spine. The bugs raced across his neck and into his cheeks, and scratching at them left his cheeks red and raw.

But the pills increased Lorn's appetite and that pleased his mother. He could hear her now, saying, "Double your dosage. Triple your dosage! If you could just gain thirty pounds, you might feel better about yourself. Do you have any idea how many people would kill to have a weight-*gain* problem? Just about everybody."

Maybe, Lorn thought, *I should* triple my dosage.

Lorn's ever-thoughtful and impressively intelligent psychiatrist—Doc Mike—believed that mothers sometimes made hyperbolic and insensitive comments. He also believed that young men did not have to do everything their mothers told them to do because young men were fully formed adults now and could make their own decisions. Doc Mike further believed that patients didn't always need medication.

Lorn heard Doc Mike's voice in his head: "We simply have to retrain your brain."

But the shaking? The blurry vision? The bugs? The pills? The appetite? Lorn weighed his choices. *Am I the cause of my own illness?* he wondered and gnawed on the thought, his knees clapping. *Doc Mike thinks I am the cause and the solution to all of my problems.*

Lorn shook a white pill from the prescription bottle, sat the capsule between his lips like an e-cig, and puffed once before sucking the pill into his mouth, thinking that an appetite boost would serve him well. After all, wasn't Doc Mike always saying that infirmed young men needed to maintain their appetites? Lorn already ate plenty—bacon burgers, alfredo pastas, sandwiches stacked half a foot high, oozing cheese and mayonnaise—but he never gained weight. The oversized shirts he wore concealed a concave chest, protruding ribs, and hip bones whose points bulged at his waistline.

Three years ago, just before Lorn took his driving test, his lung collapsed. Spontaneous pneumothorax, doctors called it, a rather common condition for the very tall, very thin, and very frail. Lorn was all of those things. He had been forbidden to leave the hospital until he gained weight, so he feasted on hospital pizza and hospital meatball subs and hospital cheese lasagna. He devoured tubs of ice cream and gallons of milkshakes, and once the doctors liked the number they saw on their digital scale, they released Lorn. Ten days later, he bombed his driving test and lost all the weight he had gained. That, and more.

∾

Lorn couldn't stay in his apartment any longer. He hated the unadorned walls, the faux-wood flooring, the tiny dust mountains collecting in the corners, and the cockroaches playing peekaboo in the kitchen sink. The stacks of moving boxes sickened him, but he refused to unpack. He preferred to live out of boxes rather than admit that this lousy apartment was home. He was not going to buy furniture, was not going to settle in, was not going to get comfortable.

Most weekends, despite his jitters, Lorn visited a nearby park and walked circles around the lake. The walks calmed his thoughts, made him feel that all was not lost, that someday life would improve. Today, however, a cold front had stalled over the city, and rain showers persisted, so, instead of the park, Lorn would visit Valley View, the old mall.

Since La Grande Expérience opened—complete with a Playtorium and an ice-skating rink—few people patronized Valley View. Just a year ago, Boscov's and JCPenney closed, and no other retailers replaced them. The electronics and jewelry stores closed. The sporting goods and clothing stores closed. Then the high schoolers disappeared. After all, who needed a mall these days—the crowds, the lines, the fight for parking—when one could buy everything online?

Before his collapsed lung, before medication, Lorn worked part-time at a Valley View shoe store on the second level. He had chafed at the manager's rules: tucked-in, collared shirt; name tag; and dress shoes with matching leather belt. He had taken the job thinking he would love caressing young women's tender soles, but he was surprised and dismayed by how many pretty women had smelly feet. But he had kept the job for the money. During downtime, Lorn logged new inventory, and when the manager asked for tallies, Lorn replied with genus, species, and quantity: "Boots, cowgirl, twenty-five pairs; heels, platform, thirty pairs; flats, ballerina, fifteen pairs." The store, which catered to a female clientele, also carried a selection of men's footwear: oxfords, loafers, docksiders, and chukkas among them, and if a single pair of black, size fourteen Dr. Martens went missing, the manager would never know. The shoe store had gone out of business even before Lorn graduated high school.

Lorn stepped off the 11:25 bus, bent at the curb, and, though quivering, tied his scuffed and battered old Docs, his favorite footwear. He entered Valley View Mall from the west entrance and rode a clunky escalator to the second level. Down on the first floor, a dilapidated Santa's Workshop remained, accompanied by a plastic tree wrapped in fritzing, spasmodic lights, which were more likely to cause seizures than yuletide joy. Santa had not been seen for three years. As well, steel shutters covered most storefronts on the second floor—the perfume store, the furniture store, the candle store.

Lorn traversed the mall not to shop but to exhaust the bugs prancing under his skin. When he tired, the bugs tired, and that brought relief. Lorn bypassed the escalator and descended the stairs. Heart rattling, he blazed across the first level to the food court, the only vibrant part of the dying mall, where the air smelled of salt and oil, fried chicken and spicy tacos, beef patties and sweet and sour sauce. The ice cream shop—Dreamery Creamery—glowed white and cool. As Lorn passed, the food court sizzled with activity: beeping fryers and microwaves, scurrying staff, chattering diners on lunch break, chiming cash registers. The food court alone kept Valley View alive.

Midway through the third lap around the mall, Lorn's ankle radiated pain. He had been suffering from a strained Achilles for months. The discomfort steadily increased, but Lorn preferred this ailment to the bugs under his skin. For one, doctors could see strains and tears, but bugs never appeared on X-rays or MRIs. Lorn slowed. He had intended to complete ten full laps of the mall, but the sore Achilles refused.

At the same time, hunger struck Lorn suddenly, vociferously. He heard his mother say, "Thirty pounds would do you good." But Lorn wished he weren't hungry now, at noon, with the food court lines squirming away from the registers like snakes' tails. A sign at the burger joint promised: "The quickest service; the tastiest burgers." Lorn joined the line, which, ten minutes later, still had not moved. Behind the counter, the team of burger servers had dwindled to one employee. The chubby-cheeked girl wore a burger hat splashed with the orange-and-brown franchise logo. She jabbed a finger at the register, took orders and money, gave back receipts and boxed burgers. She pulled baskets of fries out of the fryer, shook them, salted them, and while the oil dripped, she submerged other baskets of fries. Next, she flipped pink patties on the griddle and readied buns before hurrying back to the register.

Lorn eyed the blurry menu posted high above the counter. The options overwhelmed him, and he had to change his stance to keep his knees from knocking. Excessive choice made Lorn nervous. Life would be easier if restaurants served just one meal. Customers wouldn't have to order, wouldn't have to talk to the chubby-cheeked girl behind the counter who was cute but would never date a tall, thin, frail, jittering weirdo. His eye rested on the double pattie melt: three words, five syllables. He could say that much.

The line chugged forward. Money ready, Lorn silently rehearsed: *double pattie melt, double pattie melt. Remember to smile,* he thought. *Say, "Double pattie melt," hand over the money, and smile.* The chubby-cheeked girl called, "Next." Lorn panicked and stepped out of line. *I don't want a burger,* he told himself.

He moved to the back of a new line. Tacos: one word, two syllables, and Lorn could linger at the toppings bar and dress his tacos any way he liked, and that thought eased his anxiety. The tacos line inched forward. Lorn scratched the bugs under his forearms and neck, inflaming the skin and scattering the crawly things, which regrouped in his stomach. The bugs somersaulted, cartwheeled, and leaped, and Lorn pressed a palm to his abdomen. The bugs were hungry, too.

Lorn studied the taco menu. The family value pack—four tacos, four large sodas, and four sides—appealed to him. He hated onion rings but the cheese-drizzled potato tots looked appetizing. The people ahead of Lorn placed orders with enviable ease. A father moved his young daughter forward, her chin no higher than the counter. "Tell the server your order," the father said. The girl cleared her throat and, with authority, said, "I want a soft taco, fully loaded, and for my sides, I want beans and rice, please." The girl placed her palms on the counter and rhythmically tapped her fingertips. "Oh, and I want a pink lemonade. Hold the ice, please."

Before his lung collapsed, Lorn had been just as confident, and though his lung recovered, his confidence did not.

The father pushed money into his daughter's hand. She paid, received change and her order, and, grinning, followed her father to an empty table.

"Next."

"Your turn, pal," the man behind Lorn said.

Lorn forgot his order. He felt the impatience of the people around him, those in line, those behind the counter. The bugs choked him, and he pawed at his throat but could not speak. With a jittery side-step, Lorn took himself out of line. Hadn't the last five years been like that—indecision, anxiety, and escape?

Lorn kept moving—moving sometimes masked his jitters and con-fused the bugs—and joined the end of the Chinese food line. The over-head menu included white-washed pictures of favorite dishes: moo shu chicken, Hunan pork, and beef chow mein. The pale, unappeal-ing, blurry images troubled Lorn. He thought he might order what-ever was cheapest or most popular. Maybe he would slide some bills across the counter and ask the cashier to "gimme whatever." The line for Chinese food moved as slowly as all of the other lines, but now Lorn was thankful for the delay. Despite protests from the bugs in his stomach, Lorn rested, gathered himself, spoke calm affirmations to himself the way Doc Mike instructed.

Back when Lorn worked at the mall shoe store, he dined regularly at the food court and ordered without difficulty. He used to com-mandeer the counter and place his order like a normal person.

As the line shortened, Lorn's nervousness increased. The sweet 'n sour chicken was easy enough to pronounce. He practiced. *"Yes. I'd like the sweet 'n sour chicken. Thank you."* He'd hand over the money and say, *"Keep the change,"* and the disbelieving cashier would be happy and grateful and consider Lorn a cool guy, and Lorn would laud his own kindness and humanitarianism. His appetite, then, would burst forth, and he would eat and gain weight and finally feel normal.

By the time Lorn reached the front of the line, he'd been at the food court for almost an hour, and the bugs under his skin raged. Lorn boldly stepped to the counter and came face to face with a pale dumpling wearing a smock and a name tag. Ashley had small eyes and a slouching lip like a boxer. She spoke like a boxer, too. "Well, you gonna order or what?" Her yellow teeth matched the color of the crusts in the corners of her eyes. The oily girl needed a long, thorough shower. Lorn stepped out of line, awash in failure and dis-appointment. If he couldn't place an order, he couldn't eat, and the bugs would rage on. He considered leaving the mall but didn't. What would he do in his unadorned apartment but watch rainwater play upon the bedroom window? If he went to his mother's house, she would feed him, but he would have to listen to her ridicule. "What do you mean you couldn't order a burger at the food court?" He heard Doc Mike say, "We will never overcome our fears if we don't face them. To avoid or to quit is easy, but where is the growth in that?"

Lorn straightened his posture, forced his shoulders back and his chest forward. Pizza-rama's line curled around a pillar and past the seating area. Customers departed the counter, coveting triangular boxes and sodas with straws poking out of them like antennae. They found seating, threw back the box lids, and, holding high their gooey, oily slices, chomped the pointed tips. Cheesy ribbons stretched and snapped and brought smiles to faces.

Pizza was the perfect order: no drink, no toppings, no sides; a hulking slice at a cheap price; simple and easy. Lorn would hardly have to order to get his triangular box. He joined the back of the line and soon found himself behind professionally attired people his own age. The young men and women wore shirts with collars and pressed slacks. Belts matched shoes. The women sported low-heel ankle boots or T-strap Mary Janes while the men donned loafers or lace-up oxfords. They smelled like the perfume store before it closed.

Their voices rang loudly in Lorn's ears as they pontificated on pop stars and video games and celebrity gossip. They spoke unfiltered, believing that everything they said was important, hilarious, necessary, and brilliant, and that, if they didn't speak, the world would somehow be diminished. They texted while they talked, necks curving toward tiny screens, thumbs jabbing away. Even as they professed and proclaimed, they heard none but their own voice. Lorn likened the group to a broken soda fountain in which every variety gushed forth simultaneously. Lorn, on the other hand, measured and rehearsed his words before speaking them. If these young businessmen and women were gushing soda fountains, what was Lorn?

Without looking away from their phones, the group ahead of Lorn placed its order. They waved their phones near the register until a chime sounded and a "Thank you for your business" appeared on the register's digital screen. They carried their pizzas to a vacant table.

As always, Lorn practiced his order: *"A slice, please. A slice, please."*
But when the cashier looked up at him, Lorn's stomach clenched.
"A slice," he managed to say, but as the cashier turned from the counter to fetch the pizza, Lorn scuttled away, sick with nervousness. Bugs
flopped under his skin. His belly moaned. The cashier called from
behind, "Hey, your pizza." Lorn's cheeks burned with embarrassment;
sweat slicked his neck, and he had already walked too far away to go
back. If he stopped, if he turned around, how many people would he
find staring at him, wondering terrible things about him, asking themselves what was wrong with that very tall, very thin, very frail guy?

Lorn retreated to a vacant corner of the food court, to the border-
land between the lively food court and the moribund mall. Hunger
persisted, as did frustration, but he could not complete the ordering
process. His jitters increased, and the bugs rebelled. And Lorn felt like
he had in the moments before his lung collapsed.

He had been sixteen, friendless, with bangs falling into his eyes,
selling shoes to women whose feet smelled. His mother had just
won the house from his estranged father. His guidance counselor had
just been diagnosed with prostate cancer that had metastasized to his
hip, lungs, and brain. During a meeting in the guidance office, Mr.
Bell confided to Lorn that "Nothing matters, not kindness, not spite,
not revenge or charity. For some reason, we are here"—he began to
sniffle and tear—"and then we are not here. Who cares about college
entrance exams? You might not make it that far." Shortly after, Mr.
Bell began using his bank of sick and vacation days and never came
back to school.

Lorn's jitters began one morning and would not quit. He struggled
to keep cereal on his spoon as he ate breakfast. His chest burned and,
while carrying his bowl to the kitchen sink, he became short of breath
and collapsed. He struggled for air, thinking all the while about Mr.
Bell. The old bastard had been right; life *was* fleeting and pointless.

Lorn jerked out of the memory, clawing at the bugs that had rallied
in the center of his chest, demanding sustenance. *A line*, Lorn thought,
he had to find another line. Lines afforded him hope, the possibility
that he could place an order and see it through. Lines gave him the

semblance of company, proximity to other people without commitment to them. In line, he participated in the human experience. But once he reached a counter, he had to choose, to decide. At a counter, the moment fell upon him: the attention, the pressure, the feeling that his lung once again would collapse. Had Mr. Bell felt a similar pressure at the moment of his cancer diagnosis?

Hunger weakened Lorn and empowered the bugs. For the bulk of his life, he had stood on plenty of lines, placed plenty of orders, paid for and eaten plenty of meals. But everything about this day conspired against him, and the weaker he became, the harder it would be to satisfy his appetite.

~

Lorn had been in the food court for more than ninety minutes, long enough for the lunchtime rush to end. Now, shorter lines remained and relieved cashiers patrolled their stations. Food court tables sat empty as diners bussed their trays and exited the mall.

Dreamery Creamery—like a beacon—caught Lorn's attention, its pink-and-white motif pleasantly captivating, its joyous crew fluttering behind the counter. Just two people waited in line. *Ice cream could save the day*, Lorn thought, *only ice cream*. The calories and fat would strengthen him; the sugar shock would embolden him, and the bugs would be pleased, even delighted.

Lorn stood at the back of the line, hiding his jittery hands in his pockets, eager for a cool treat, wondering if he should order the classic chocolate chip or try something new. While recovering from his collapsed lung, Lorn had developed a hankering for Chocolate Nut Blast and Extreme Praline Pie. One thing was certain; he would not order Rum RaiSin, his mother's favorite flavor. The taste sickened him.

The summer before sixth grade, when the multiplex still operated, Lorn and his mother visited Valley View weekly for the half-price matinees. Usually, mother and son had their choice of seats in the empty theater, and just before the feature played, his mother would lean over and whisper, "This is like our own private theater." Together, they cheered heroes or flinched when monsters burst onscreen. And if the movie satisfied, they would stand and applaud as the credits rolled. Afterward, his mother would whisper again. "Let's be naughty. What do you say?" At the food court, Lorn would order a double-scoop cone, his mother a cup of Rum RaiSin.

Lorn never thought the mall would die and take his memories with it.

He sidled to the display case and glared down at the five-gallon tubs of ice cream, entranced by the colors: mint green, vanilla white, raspberry red, fudge brown, and birthday blue. Though dazzled by the colors, Lorn again cringed at the multitude of options.

Two girls behind the counter—they might have been sisters—featured identical ponytails and ill-fitting uniforms that pulled against their ample busts and hips and sagged everywhere else. They wore plastic gloves stained with caramel, butterscotch, and strawberry sauces. Like ballroom dancers, the girls worked in tandem, stepping, twirling, sliding, anticipating the other's moves, communicating solely with winks and nods. For all of their similarities, the girls' faces marked a divergence. One girl exhibited a low-hanging bulbous nose book-ended by cheeks so plump they threatened to swallow her mouth. The second girl's mouth slouched to one side of a narrow face that somehow maintained a generous double chin.

Lorn rehearsed his order. He had to eat something and soon; otherwise, he would never get to his next dosage of medication. Lorn channeled his mother; she had never botched a post-matinee order, and now she would help him. Lorn advanced and anchored himself to the counter. He would order a double-scoop cone. "Let's be naughty," he heard his mother say. "Make it a triple dose."

The girl with the narrow face and double chin waited on Lorn. "So many choices," Lorn said, his mouth suddenly parched. Bugs charged from his chest into his throat, and if he didn't order swiftly, the critters might spill out of his mouth and across the counter, their hairy legs scrabbling upon the stainless steel. "Cone," he said quickly and pushed money at the girl.

"What?"

"Please. A cone," he repeated.

"Flavor?"

"Chocolate chip. Triple dose." Lorn immediately sealed his mouth.

The girl gave him change and a receipt and filled the order. "Here you go." She carefully put the cone into his hand, said, "Napkins are there," and called the next customer forward.

He had done it. He had placed an order and seen it through. Lorn savored his accomplishment. But the jitters persisted and the bugs frenzied just behind his lips. He feared a mass insect exodus. Already, the triple stack of ice cream sweated and dripped, and Lorn wrapped the cone in napkins. Ice cream rivulets dribbled over the lip of the cone and down its shaft, pooling in the web between his forefinger and thumb. The scoops wobbled atop the cone as his jitters and vision worsened and the bugs stomped. Now, melting ice cream surmounted his knuckles and streaked the back of his hand. Ice cream droplets dotted the mall floor, tracing Lorn's shaky journey from the food court into the dying mall. Shuttered shops lined the corridor. Behind their security gates lay empty and partially disassembled display cases and shelves. Red and green wires dangled from ceiling tiles where lighting fixtures had hung.

The bugs wailed for sustenance. The top scoop of ice cream came loose and splattered to the floor. Lorn shuddered. His lungs twitched, anticipating a complete collapse. He struggled for air. The second scoop rolled away when Lorn raised the cone to his lips. He pushed his mouth into the last soggy remains of his ice cream cone, tongued the cool, creamy goo, and spat Rum RaiSin.

The Dreamery Creamery girl had bungled the order.

Unable to steady himself, Lorn dropped the cone and crashed against one shop's security gate, blurry-eyed, starving, and feeling that at any moment his lung would collapse, and like the mall itself he'd slowly suffocate, die, and be forgotten.

THE HERO'S EMBRACE

I'M NOT SURE HOW ZIP-LINING forty yards into Hyman Lowenstein's awaiting arms is supposed to make me a better employee. This is another dumb idea that won't work. Look at Hyman down there, his pale and thin arms spread wide to catch me in what our instructor calls the Hero's Embrace. Meanwhile, I'm three stories high and 120 feet away; Hyman's going to need an anchor and a coat of armor to keep me from zip-lining a hole right through his scrawniness. And did anyone (Mr. Instructor) take into account the wind conditions today? It's gusting toward a nor'easter and doom is in the air.

The others in my group have zipped already: one of the secretaries, half of the brilliant and obnoxious interns, an assistant director. Antonius didn't give us a choice. So here I am, forced to leap.

The helmet—some padding inside a plastic shell—is flimsy, the fit tenuous, the straps loose. Shouldn't I have a face guard of some kind, elbow pads, gloves, a harness? The instructor steps behind me onto the ledge. My toes spider forward; my hands grip the trolley handlebar above my head.

On the landing platform below stand my office mates, some shielding their eyes, perhaps some wishing the cable will snap or Hyman Lowenstein will panic and I'll get flattened. Why does Antonius devise these team-building activities?

A few of the passive-aggressive interns hold up their phones to record me.

The instructor says, "Don't look down and don't think. Just jump."
I freeze.

If Hyman drops me, I'll kill him. If the wind kinks the cable and I get hung up and the fire department has to save me, I'll kill the instructor. If anything rotten happens, I'll sue, starting with Antonius.

Antonius bounds onto the ledge, elbowing the instructor aside. His head hangs over my shoulder, his mouth at my ear. "You will jump, Melvin, because you're part of this team. Rogues are unwelcome."

I don't move.

"Accept that you are afraid." Antonius sounds like an emperor. "Fear not! Lowenstein is loyal to the team. Trust he'll catch you."

I am not afraid. I've biked Grand Fork Mountain, climbed El Mesa del Dios, speed-hiked out of Soup Bowl Canyon, and zip-lined through the Costa Rican rainforest during a monsoon.

"Why can't you be more like Lowenstein?" Antonius asks, still breathing into my ear. He hip-checks me and my feet fly off the ledge.

As the instructor demonstrated, I raise my knees toward my chest, hang by my arms in a semi-seated position. Wind whips past my ears as the zipline trolley buzzes the cable. The platform comes into view; the others have moved back and away from Hyman Lowenstein. Smartphones track my flight. I near, faster, faster. Hyman braces, arms wide, knees bent, what's left of his hair shivering in the breeze. His miniscule lips turn white; his tie flies back over one shoulder. (Hyman's the only one so primly dressed.)

The platform shoots beneath me as I lower my legs, creating drag, hoping I don't pull Hyman's arms out of his shoulders when he attempts the Hero's Embrace. As my heels thump the steel grating, I sense that Lowenstein will flinch, retract his arms as if from a fierce flame, and I will slide right off the back side of the platform, drop onto the pavement, and collectively snap every bone from shoulder to toe. Before passing out from pain, I will curse Antonius.

A millisecond after touchdown, Hyman Lowenstein's arms swaddle my waist. His head catches my sternum and we both get dragged by momentum. Hyman is stronger than he looks, smarter too. He lowers his center of gravity, making himself a pale, freckled mooring.

His grip doubles, and before another second passes, he and I are in the
Hero's Embrace, staring at each other, safe on the platform.

The passive-aggressive interns lower their phones, upset that they
don't have a colossal fail for web upload. The pair of secretaries sar-
castically cheers us.

Back on the third-story window ledge, Antonius, helmet locked in
place, bellows and hoots like a cockatoo and leaps from the ledge.
The cotton collar of his polo shirt becomes tiny wings about his neck.
He lands on the platform, no help needed. He inhales, pushing out his
chest, hands on hips. "Now, that's how you do it! Only teamwork will
make you people better; only trust will make you more productive."
Antonius commands the second team to get up to the third floor.

As we wait for our partners to zip-line, Antonius wraps an arm
around my shoulders. "Do you feel it? That's teamwork, that's collab-
oration. When you trust your cubicle mate, quality and production
grow. Be like Lowenstein."

I nod, smile, but don't feel any different. I don't suddenly respect
Antonius or trust Hyman Lowenstein or admire the assistant direc-
tors. I still dislike the moron secretaries, still hate the snooty interns.
I will continue to apply clandestinely for new jobs at better companies.

I know how to get my work done, know what elementary tasks
the interns can handle, know not to ask the secretaries for anything
because they'll just muck it up, and if I involve the assistant directors,
they'll try to take credit for my work.

And Hyman is the worst of all. Every chance he gets, Hyman sweet-
talks Antonius: "Here's the assessment document you asked for, sir. You
were right to have me color-code and laminate it. Great idea, Antonius!"

Hyman's phony flattery makes me ill.

"Who's first?" Antonius yells up to the third-floor window and
Hyman shoots his arm into the air, pushes forward, and steps onto the
ledge. "Take your place, Melvin," Antonius says to me. "Your partner
needs you."

The others on the platform leave the landing zone and I, as the instructor demonstrated, bend at the waist and knees, arms outstretched,
and rotate onto the balls of my feet.

"This is your partner," Antonius says. "Show me your team spirit!"

Hyman yanks his tie, stretches his neck. The instructor smacks Hyman's helmet, yells, "Check!" Hyman raises his stick arms, grips the handlebar, pauses long enough to flip his tie over one shoulder. "Melvin," he calls to me, "Here I come!"

Hyman leaps from the ledge, brings his knees up. The cable sings with tension as he zooms along.

Hyman is not the hardest worker in the office. Neither is Antonius. I am the one who stayed late in order to accommodate the heavy workflow last quarter. I am the one who acquired state licensure, bringing national prestige to the office. I am the one who single-handedly revamped our operations to provide a broader range of client services. Hyman is Antonius's sycophant. The secretaries, the interns, the assistant directors are noodle-spined followers.

Hyman approaches, his speed tremendous; I can see the stretch of his nose, his yellow teeth. He sails toward the platform and I am ready for the Hero's Embrace.

Antonius calls at me from outside the landing zone: "Come on, Melvin. Bend those knees, brace yourself, like Lowenstein did." The laces of Hyman's shoes, the buttons of his shirt come into focus. Antonius coaches: "Arms wider, Melvin. Here he comes."

I flash Antonius a look, can't stop thinking about how I don't belong.

"Pay attention. Whatever you do, don't let him go. Your partner is counting on you. Trust in teamwork!"

"Shut up!" I scowl at Antonius, and the secretaries flinch. Hyman is thirty feet away.

Why do I play these games? Teamwork can't be forced nor trust ordered.

"Hero's Embrace!" Antonius yells.

Hyman is thirteen feet away, six feet, two feet.

"Now, Melvin! Do it! Do it!"

I do what I should have done a long time ago, and roar, "I quit!" And as Hyman Lowenstein arrives, I stand aside and watch him fly.

LEAVING

On Christmas Eve, the Knoxville Airport was dead empty. Periodically, a recorded announcement regarding safe-travel tips played over the public address system, and somewhere out of sight a cable news station reported and re-reported nonsense: the folly of last-minute shoppers, the current Dow averages, the slate of films opening today, and the pop diva defending her latest album even as fans snatched up copies by the thousands.

Gabe Padukah threw himself into a seat, one with a direct view of Gate 10 and no view of planes taking off or landing. He wouldn't even glance out the large terminal windows because he didn't want to think about where he was.

A custodian marched her long-handled dustpan from one waiting area to the next, catching scraps of paper, candy wrappers, and old luggage tags, and dumping them into her wheeled trash can. The muffled flare of salsa sizzled through her headphones as she ambled here and there in the terminal. Gabe remembered his own pair of headphones, stuffed into the small suitcase at his feet. He didn't need them now, not with his feet still on the ground, not with an hour till boarding. If he boarded—and if he needed musical distraction at all—it would be at takeoff, to forget takeoff.

Two years ago, a prospective employer had flown Gabe to Seattle. In mid-flight, Gabe suffered a severe panic attack, which stunned him, rolling out like a frigid wave from his brain to his limbs. He'd begun shaking, gasping almost. His saliva dried and his lips stuck to his teeth. Though this had never happened before, he didn't call the flight attendant for help. Bewildered but safely arrived, Gabe regrouped and charged on to the interview. He performed well, felt good about his chances of getting hired. A hiring committee member had asked, "What is your weakness?"

"I'm too content to suffer quietly."

After the interview, Gabe Padukah had gotten on the return flight, despite his mind and body raging against it. Once in his seat, he tried to drug himself with a quartet of sleeping pills purchased at an airport gift shop. He waited and waited—through the close of the cabin door, the safety demonstration, the taxi to the runway—for the pills to work. He crunched two more pills in his back teeth, yet for the next five hours, all Gabe could do was sweat and shiver, and wait for the terrible, unstoppable panic to destroy him. Sleep could not overtake him; his body's alert system refused. However, once the plane had landed and the cabin door opened, Gabe pushed his way off, his seatback, like his shirt, drenched through. Then, in the terminal, the sleeping pills activated, and Gabe slept all afternoon on the Knoxville Airport floor. He awoke, swearing never to fly again.

Gabe had not been offered the job in Seattle.

∼

Gabe did not want to think about the last time he was on a plane. In fact, he'd been practicing forgetting the past, as one might practice meditation or sobriety. A website Gabe liked to visit had called the problem aviophobia: "You clench when you should relax. You fixate on the bad and minimize the good." The website recommended that Gabe "recognize his triggers and ignore the things that go bump in the flight (LOL)."

The custodian smiled at Gabe as she loafed past, her teeth crooked, gapped, or gone. Compelled, Gabe smiled back then eyed the book in his lap: the *Odyssey*, a hardcover edition missing its dust jacket. He read a few pages and a few pages more but tired of the characters, troubled by the constant references to lineage: Nausicaa, daughter of

Alcinous; Ktimene, sister of Odysseus; and Eperitos, son of Apheidas
and grandson of King Polypemon. Gabe squirmed in his seat, wishing never to be known through his relatives. "I am unique; my expe-
riences are unique," he told himself.

A woman with the winged emblem of an airline company on her
uniform led her roller bag down the concourse. She hid her age under
dark eye shadow and rosy blush and slipped through a security door
using the pass card dangling around her neck.

Gabe forgot Seattle, but when it wouldn't stay forgotten, he
squinched his eyes shut, reminded himself that old events were not
related to new events—especially those that hadn't happened yet—
just like ancestors had no effect on offspring. Each was independent
of the other: Gabe, son of . . . who cares? This was not Seattle; Seattle
was Seattle (and he'd survived Seattle, anyway); hence, this could never
be Seattle, and since that was true, Seattle-Gabe could not be Knoxville-
Gabe: Gabe was Gabe and could never again be Seattle-Gabe. Obvi-
ously, there were similarities between the two—airport, gate, runway,
plane, uncomfortable seats, luggage, Gabe, loads of nervousness creeping up his spine—but similar did not mean same.

Just because there was a plane and Gabe waiting to board it, that
did not mean the result would be the same. Just because his mother
had died, that did not mean . . . but that *would* be the same. Gabe
leaned down and pushed the *Odyssey* into the outer pocket of his
suitcase and removed his journal. The aviophobia website had told
Gabe that thoughts were like knickknacks and heads were like trunks,
and fliers who held onto thoughts (the bad ones) too long often had
cluttered trunks, dangerously cluttered. Under the "Treatment" tab,
the website advocated frequent journaling.

Gabe picked at the thick rubber band securing his journal as a few
passengers entered the waiting area and sat. They did not appear nervous. One passenger, who had snuck in beside Gabe, said, "That's a
wicked cover."

Gabe followed the remark to a teenaged girl with a braid sweeping across her forehead and behind one ear. She pressed an unpol-
ished fingernail to the journal. The cover itself, made from a faux

hide, contained an ancient-looking map drawn as if by the hand of Columbus's chief cartographer. The map centered on Europe. West, across the sea called Mar Del Nort, only a brief coastal outline had been drawn on a continent labeled America Septentrionalis.

Gabe scouted for the girl's parents, expecting to see two squares in pastel polo shirts scowling in his direction.

"I'm Maddie."

Gabe, as though trying to shrug off the teen, shifted in his seat.

"What's your name?" she asked.

He told her his name and she shook his hand, saying, "Nice to meet you."

When Maddie smiled, her cheeks plumped and gleaming teeth showed between pink lips. Miniscule pimples dotted her chin. "I'm flying alone," Maddie said. "It's my first time."

"That's great," Gabe said dully. He sensed a sting; strangers, especially young girls, did not just start talking to him. He proceeded cautiously. "My sister, Bianca, gave me this journal some years ago." The journal weighed over two pounds; a pen marked Gabe's place among the tan, lined pages.

"It's as thick as a double-decker cheeseburger," Maddie said.

"I've been making entries for about two years and haven't even reached the midpoint."

From her carry-on, Maddie removed a simple pocket notebook dressed with a collage of stickers cramming the front and back covers. She asked, "What do you write about, 'cause I write about, like, everything. Whatever's bothering me, stuff like that."

"Me, too."

"Will you write about this? Will you write about us meeting, how a strange girl named Maddie liked your journal?"

"I don't know."

Now, enough passengers filled the waiting area to create an audible buzz.

"I'm going to write about you," Maddie said, her grin widening. She told Gabe that New York City was her first stop, then she'd take another flight to St. Louis next week. "My grandparents, they don't get along, not since the Clinton administration, as my dad would say. You can put that in your journal, if you want."

The door to Gate 10 opened and arriving passengers filed out, trailing their roller bags behind. As the passengers whizzed by, Maddie asked, "Do you ever just, like, read back through old entries and go: 'What was I thinking? I was so stupid then, scared for no reason'?"

"No."

At Gate 9, Maddie's New York City flight started to board. "Too bad we're not on the same plane," she said. "We could read each other's journals and laugh at ourselves." As Maddie moved to the other gate, she looked back. "Safe travels."

∽

The heavily made-up flight attendant Gabe had seen earlier settled behind the Gate 10 counter and, using the intercom, announced that the Cleveland flight would board shortly. The passengers around Gabe gathered their belongings, readied their boarding passes, crowded forward.

Gabe checked his ticket: an aisle seat, toward the stern. A sparkle caught his eye; a tiny bead of sweat had pooled on his thumb. He smeared it back into his skin but another appeared, prickling forth, and now his heart started slamming against his chest. "Don't think," he reminded himself. "Relax," he reminded himself. Needing a distraction, Gabe texted Bianca: "Leaving."

The flight attendant welcomed the first-class passengers aboard.

Gabe's phone vibrated with a reply from Bianca: "Bon voyage." He tried to focus on Bianca's face, but it continually morphed into the face of their mother, dead less than a year; cancer had come and carried her out of the ICU. Until the end, his mother had sworn she was fine. In fact, she had done most of the talking that last time: "How's life in Knoxville?" "What's new at work?" "I aim to visit you one of these days. When's a good time?"

Gabe held the memory: His mother had not been fine. She had been scared of dying, sad and terrified to leave. He wished he'd said something: "Can't we get another second opinion?" "What are all these doctors doing anyway?" "Can't they just cut that lump out of your throat?"

Gabe's mother had died alone, just one hour after that last conversation. She had waited for Gabe to leave.

"Zones two and three," the flight attendant called. Vacationers and suit-wearing business travelers shuffled forward to present their tickets. Gabe Padukah stood but did not move toward the boarding line.

"I'm just not going," he told himself and wondered about buses, trains, and rental cars. He'd never make the ceremony in time. Bianca would have to understand; he had an inside illness: aviophobia. The website had insisted irrational fear was the cause. The solution was simple: "Relax."

Gabe wasn't ready to die (more irrational fear).

The line of passengers dwindled.

Gabe's thoughts persisted: nonrefundable tickets; Bianca's eternal fury at his absence. His sweaty hands worked like jaws, chewing the boarding pass. Somehow, he lurched on numb legs to the back of the line.

His mother must have experienced tremendous worry, too. She had been mad when the cancer arrived, vowed to crush it and did. But when it returned, she told no one. She'd lost twenty then thirty pounds and could no longer go to work. Her back had kept her awake every night. Then her breathing soured and she had to sleep sitting up. When she coughed, veins lined her face. Thick mucus choked her.

Gabe let a family of latecomers go ahead of him. He knelt beside his suitcase, opening pockets, rifling through them, repeating a prayer. He pushed aside his headphones, dug into the corners of each pocket until, finally, he pulled free a loop of cheap plastic rosary beads. They had been one of many pairs hanging from his mother's hospital bed.

All other passengers had boarded. Gabe clenched the beads, asked to forget.

"Young man? Sir?" the flight attendant called. "Are you on this flight?"

Gabe said nothing and didn't budge. His ticket was a soggy, wrinkled leaf unwinding on the floor.

Could it be, Gabe wondered, that a person, having lived a long life, felt ready to die? His mother had raised two children virtually by herself; they turned out to be hard workers and decent people, self-sufficient and urbane. Perhaps his mother had known this and, content, was ready to reunite with relatives and friends, to see her own parents: Mom, daughter of Carl and Sue.

"Sir, if you're getting on this flight, the time is now."

His knees bent, his feet rose and planted, each leg catching his weight. The air around Gabe Padukah moved; he did not retreat but advanced. He relinquished the mangled boarding pass; the flight attendant smoothed it against the countertop and scanned it.

Gabe looked across to Gate 9 and spotted Maddie. She waved her arm overhead, in her hand a sticker-covered journal.

"Sir," the flight attendant said, handing back the creased ticket. "It's time, sir."

"I'm ready." Gabe, before entering the tunnel, waved to Maddie.

"Enjoy your trip, sir."

~

The light in the jetway came from electric bulbs cased in thick plastic. Gabe's entire body turned cold. The plane waited at the end of the jetway. A flight attendant welcomed Gabe aboard and, hunching low, he weaseled his way through the cabin to his seat.

He wanted to get off the plane or wanted someone to knock him unconscious. This time he'd packed Dramamine tablets and chewed them two at a time. The vaguely orange flavor reminded him of children's vitamins. The cabin door shut, and Gabe's chest constricted. His breathing labored; his stomach knotted. He swung his headphones over his ears and hit play, hoping the songs would transport him. Gabe shut his eyes rather than watch the safety demonstration.

He told himself lies: that he was not on a plane, that his heart was not galloping, that this was not like Seattle, that he was not panicking.

The plane jerked once before rolling back from the gate and turning toward the runway. Gabe pictured himself in a dark, safe womb, but the image crumbled. He cranked the music louder and opened his journal, leafing back several pages, through months, years. He skimmed passages about Bianca first announcing her pregnancy, then giving birth, then asking Gabe to come to Cleveland and serve as godfather. He read about his mother's funeral, how she was no longer suffering in the ICU, no longer choking on mucus. And last he read about waking in the Knoxville Airport, how he swore he'd never fly again because he didn't want to die.

"What was I thinking?" Gabe said to himself. "I was so stupid then, scared for no reason."

The plane turned; the turbines surged louder and louder, and Gabe was knocked back in his seat. The plane tilted as the front wheel leaped off the runway.

And in his lap, Gabe found his journal already opened to a new page, the pen already in hand, the first line already written: "This strange girl named Maddie said she liked my journal."

THE SISTERS

Since about 1955, the Brooklyn kids had been calling Kathy and her older sister, Maura, "the Irish Twins." All the neighborhood knew that the sisters, born eleven months apart, were not actually twins, but the moniker, a harmless tease, stuck. Kathy, sixteen, and Maura, seventeen, both had vibrant blue eyes, brown hair curling to the shoulder, and generous smiles. Kathy loved that she and Maura were the same size and swapped dresses, shoes, skirts, and tops. But she also recognized that she and Maura were different in significant ways. For one, Kathy had fair skin and freckles on her arms and hands, over her nose, and sprinkled across her cheeks, and in summer she typically turned pink while Maura cultivated a rich tan. Kathy was also deaf—had been since seventh grade—but read lips and spoke with only the gentlest, slightest slur.

In personality, Maura was the stoic, mature in demeanor, focused, and intent on adding good to the world. Kathy noticed in herself indecision and uncertainty; she was unsure of who and what she wanted to become. In just the last two or three years, she had considered careers as a chef, a pianist, a mother, a teacher, a biologist, and even a reporter. Because of this uncertainty, Kathy regularly interrogated Maura about her future, trying, in effect, to understand her own choices through her older sister's choices.

"I have been watching Mom," Maura admitted.

"What does that have to do with anything?" Kathy asked, impatient.

Their mother excelled as household manager and caregiver. "You can see," Maura said, as if offering a philosophical proof, "that Mom loves being a mom, like she was *called* to motherhood."

Kathy nodded. She had to admit—now that Maura pointed it out—that their mother was patient, kind, and selfless. "But what are *you* going to do after high school? What's your calling?"

Maura wrinkled her nose. "Well, I don't want to be a mother myself, not exactly."

Kathy tugged Maura's arm, thinking she had misread her sister's lips. She flipped the fingers of one hand into the palm of the other, the sign for "again."

Maura said, "Most of our friends will marry and start families. I want something else."

～

Straight through the afternoon, Kathy clandestinely monitored Maura, seeking clues to her older sister's plans. Kathy knew Maura well enough to know that if an announcement was forthcoming, it would happen at dinner, before the entire family. Their mother settled a bowl of buttered peas on the table and, tucking her skirt, sat. Kathy and the others blessed themselves, said grace, and filled their dinner plates, and when these rituals finished, Kathy watched a light come into Maura's eyes.

"I have something to tell you," Maura said to everyone. "I am joining the convent."

For several seconds, no one moved. Tingles danced over Kathy's face; she lowered her fork. Then, a slow smile bent her father's lips, and her mother dabbed her eyes with a napkin. Her parents rushed to Maura's side to kiss and congratulate her. Already, her mother was thinking about relatives she would call, letters she would send to Ireland sharing the glorious news. Kathy's brothers, though too young to comprehend fully the magnitude of the moment, pitched well-wishes across the table. Kathy crossed her arms and frowned.

Her mother extended the thumb and pinky of her fist and, with a slight headshake, touched the fist to her chin, signing, "What's wrong?" then adding, "Didn't you hear Maura's announcement?"

Kathy directed her grimace at Maura. She wasn't jealous or angry; a more complicated and nuanced emotion roiled under her flesh. "Are you sure about this, Maura?"

"I have asked myself that very question countless times, and I prayed on it, and I am sure," Maura signed and said, "very sure."

Dinner continued, and soon Kathy's scowl gave way to a look of respect and admiration. Upon reflection, Kathy surmised that she had not been upset about Maura's decision but about her own uncertainties.

~

In early summer, 1959, Maura graduated from St. Mary's Academy, turned eighteen, and put one suitcase in the Chevy's trunk. She wore a demure peach dress with a wide skirt and the same saddle shoes she wore to church and school. Because the July weather was so pristine, the traffic in Queens and Long Island was awful, especially around the airport, and the two-hour trip lasted nearly three hours. After exiting the Southern State Parkway, their father cruised through several identical-looking municipalities until their mother called out the turn-off. The black Chevy rolled between two stone pillars connected by a high, iron arch bearing the letters S.R.M., and in passing through the gate, the passengers fell silent. Acres of immaculately kept lawns spread before them. On one parcel of the sprawling grounds, a team of women in wide-brimmed hats and dungarees trimmed grass and collected and bound dead branches.

On the downslope of a minor hill, Kathy and the others watched a steeple come in to view. At its peak, set against the blue sky, stood a cross planted upon a small dome, which gave way to an ornamental belfry and elongated brick tower. Everyone in the car, including Kathy's young brothers, made the sign of the cross. A cluster of buildings— yellow brick capped with dark-claret roofs—appeared next, and their father aimed the Chevy in that direction. He parked on a strip of blacktop reserved for visitors.

The weight of the moment fell upon Kathy as she got out of the vehicle and gazed up at the buildings, which could have been state university buildings. No, Kathy amended her impression, this place was far more eminent and intimidating than some college campus. Maura showed no signs of apprehension.

Her mother beckoned her two brothers to hold her hand while her father unloaded Maura's suitcase. The family walked toward the stone steps that led to the main building's front door. Kathy drifted back, acknowledging the enormity of their sacred surroundings. As the family made its way, the front door opened and out poured a young girl in a checked skirt and pearl sweater with the sleeves rolled to the elbows. Not more than twenty years old, Kathy guessed, the girl carried a white purse and a suitcase and hurried down the steps like a cat that has just survived a wicked fight. She whimpered, tears streaking her cheeks, and came to a stop on the last step. For a moment, Kathy lingered, studying the girl and pointing her out to Maura, before following her family into the building.

A different young woman sat behind a counter in the lobby. "Name, please," she said to Kathy, who went white with shock. "Oh, I'm not . . . my sister . . ." she stuttered, quickly stepping out of the way. Maura moved forward, gave her name, and the young woman drew a finger down the list in her ledger. She ticked off Maura's name. "Sign here, please." Maura signed the ledger and returned the pen. "Maura Moloney, I am Eileen Cecilia Brosnan. Welcome to Sisters of Regina Mater Convent." She extended her hand. "Where are you from?"

"Brooklyn."

Eileen's eyebrows came together.

Maura's father leaned in. "Sligo."

"My family is from Kerry," Eileen said and grinned brightly.

Eileen Cecilia Brosnan explained that the general superior, Sister Constance, greeted all aspirants individually upon arrival. "Please, be seated," Eileen said and directed the family to a bank of chairs where other families sat. "There is a fountain down the hall if you are thirsty."

They thanked Eileen and shuffled toward the chairs, except for Kathy, who said to Eileen, "There is a girl outside, crying on the steps."

"You must mean Bridget."

"She looked pretty upset."

"God has other plans for Bridget."

One by one, girls heard their names called and entered the general superior's office alone. Kathy sat beside Maura, occasionally nudging her and directing her attention to one thing or another—the carved crucifix around Eileen's neck, the picturesque evergreens outside the hallway window, the framed paintings of Christ and Pope John XXIII affixed to the wall.

Kathy scratched two slightly bent fingers on the back of the opposite hand, the sign for "nervous."

Maura shook her head.

Kathy drooped her pointer fingers toward the floor and wagged her right hand, the sign for "very nervous."

Maura signed back: "Leave me alone."

But Kathy was overfilled with nervous energy and persisted. "What if the general superior is mean?" Kathy signed. "I bet she wields a cane and delights in scolding, threatening, and frightening new girls. Are you still sure about all of this?"

Maura resisted the preconceived notions of a cantankerous, grizzled authoritarian. "I bet she's kind, God-fearing, and motherly."

"Then why does your leg keep bobbing?"

～

Maura rose when her name was called and entered the office carrying a folder. The dimly lit room drew its light from a single, high window. Sister Constance shook Maura's hand, accepted the folder, and invited her to sit. Upon the desk lay a stack of similar folders from the girls who had gone before Maura. The woman in the full habit could not have been more than fifty years old and looked much younger with her smooth, taut cheeks and dark, chestnut bangs showing around the head covering. She needed no cane to exert her authority, moving instead with a daintiness that nonetheless exuded a quiet power.

Maura sat, knees pressed together, hands folded, back straight, and watched Sister Constance browse the folder's contents: a résumé, school transcripts, an admission application, and a letter of intent. Sister Constance scanned the letter, her blue eyes going gray. "You wrote that you want to be 'a mother to the community.'"

"Yes, Sister."

"What does that mean?"

"Sister Constance, I am open to God's mission for me."

"Would you teach?"

"Yes."

"Nurse?"

"Yes."

Sister Constance did not raise her voice in the slightest and certainly was not picking a fight, but the intensity in her eyes and behind her questions burned. "Would you evangelize? Feed the hungry? Tend to orphans and addicts and convicts?"

"Yes, Sister, if that is God's—"

"Counsel girls—many younger than you are—who have become pregnant?"

Sister Constance exuded concentrated, serious passion when she spoke, a tone befitting the general superior of Regina Mater Convent. The woman epitomized one who hears God's word and lives His commands. This meeting was not a debate but an evaluation, Maura realized. All Sister Constance wanted from aspirants was passion for the Lord. "Well, Maura Moloney? Well?"

"Yes, Sister!" Maura said with enough verve to brighten the office. "Through Christ, I can do all things."

"Is the decision to become a nun yours alone?"

Maura locked eyes with Sister Constance and would not blink; the fierceness of the expression was all the answer Sister Constance needed. She closed Maura's folder and placed it on the desk, apart from the other folders.

∼

Girls aspiring to become nuns and their families crowded into the dining hall for lunch. As the Moloneys traversed the hallway, Kathy signed to Maura. "How was the meeting with the general superior? Were you scared?"

"No," Maura signed back. "I am answering my calling."

"You might become known one day," Kathy signed and swept one hand with two extended fingers across the palm of the other hand, the sign for "saint."

Maura scoffed at the thought.

Kathy pulled near and whispered. "Imagine: If we were the same age, if we really were twins, maybe I would join the convent with you."

"Are you thinking of becoming a nun, Kathy?"

"Sure. Why not?" It was an easy response, one that caused Maura's eyes to bloom with excitement, and that made Kathy feel good. She wanted her sister to think highly of her.

"I would love to have you here with me, for us to do this together, but your decisions are between you and the Lord. Sisterhood is not like becoming a chef or a reporter."

During lunch, families ate heartily and mingled, and after dessert was served and coffee poured and sipped, Sister Constance stood at a podium, led a closing prayer, and wished families safe travels home. For the next six months, aspirants would live cloistered, confined to convent grounds and prohibited from family contact. They would begin a regimen of deep prayer and cultivate an intimate relationship with God.

Sister Constance gave a signal, and a procession of forty or fifty sisters, each carrying a lighted candle, entered the dining hall singing a hymn. The women's voices lifted and expanded, washing through the hall like string instruments and echoing back from the lofty, scalloped ceiling. The sisters positioned themselves beside every table, and when the chorus arrived, they sang directly to the aspirants:

Gentle woman, quiet light,
Morning star, so strong and bright,
Gentle Mother, peaceful dove,
Teach us wisdom; teach us love.

Sister Constance signaled the singers and their volume decreased. Families gathered a last time around their daughters, gave kisses and hugs, wept with dignity, and began to leave. Kathy, still breathless from the ceremony, did not want to leave Maura so soon. Her parents huddled around Maura. Her father kissed Maura's forehead; her mother kissed and pinched her cheeks. "I am so proud of you," her mother said, eyes watering. "We'll be back for the Christmas Eve Vigil Mass." After her brothers hugged Maura, Kathy stepped forward, emotion pooling in her eyes. The sisters embraced, and stepping back, Kathy signed, "Miss you already."

The singers offered their flickering candles to aspirants and encouraged them to sing along. Sister Constance signaled again, and the hymn swelled louder and louder. Maura took the candle given to her and joined in song. Kathy read the lyrics on her sister's lips and felt the rhythm against her flesh. Finally, as the hymn faded to a hum and as families exited, Sister Constance accosted Kathy and Maura.

"Who do we have here?"

"Sister Constance, this is my sister Kathy."

The nun smiled enthusiastically and shook Kathy's hand. Kathy's arms blushed, her nervousness immediately apparent. "For a moment, I thought you two were twins."

"Everybody thinks that," Kathy blurted and regretted opening her mouth.

"I wonder," Sister Constance went on without acknowledging Kathy's nervous energy. "Why haven't you joined the convent, too?"

Kathy struggled to make a cogent reply; Maura rescued her, saying, "Kathy is still in high school; she's a year behind me."

"But, Kathy, do you share Maura's passion for the religious life?"

Kathy, embarrassed and self-conscious, made a flurry of signs soliciting her older sister's help, but Sister Constance was called away and the conversation ended. Kathy hastened to her parents across the dining hall. She looked back a last time and signed "I love you" to Maura, who returned the gesture.

The car ride home was quiet. Straightaway, Kathy's young brothers fell asleep in the back seat. Her mother sidled beside her father as he

drove; they held hands but said nothing. Kathy, lulled by the hum of
the Chevy's tires on the highway, watched towns and hamlets pass
away, all the while swallowing back sorrow. Six months: Kathy had
never been separated from Maura for so long.

~

Now that parents and families had left the grounds, the convent settled into a decidedly monastic state with quiet activities and hushed
conversations. A regiment of women tidied the entire dining hall,
working quickly and in silence. Eileen Cecilia Brosnan and some other
women distributed room keys and invited the two dozen aspirants
to visit their new living quarters. Eileen handed Maura a key. "Would
you mind being my roommate?" she said.

Maura gladly accepted, happy to have already made a friend.

Eileen Cecilia Brosnan had recently completed her postulancy and,
in this her third year at the convent, started novitiate training. She could
not have been happier. "I don't know what I would be doing otherwise," she told Maura as they climbed the dormitory staircase. "From
very early on, probably since second grade, I knew I wanted to become a nun. I don't know; the feeling was always inside of me. Either
you know or you don't, I think." Eileen would not turn twenty-one
for another two months. She worked five days a week at the welcome
desk and loved the job. "I am part secretary, part greeter, part clerk,
and I answer the phones and take messages."

Seeking advice, Maura said, "What should I know that I don't
know?"

Eileen Cecilia Brosnan thought for a moment until one eyebrow
lifted. "I would say, be open, be curious, and be honest with yourself.
If you think this is not the life for you, then it is not the life for you.
You can't partially become a nun."

The rooms were small, unadorned, save for a single crucifix nailed to
the smoke-white cinderblock walls. Hand-stitched curtains dressed the
window. The furniture consisted of two twin beds, two small dressers,
two wardrobes, and two desks. A striped throw rug separated Eileen's
side from Maura's. The window looked out upon the expansive front

lawn, bisected by blacktop roadways, and far beyond lay a small, roofed structure. Maura squinted. "Is that a cottage? How cute."

"No, that's a shed." Eileen pointed. "Do you see? We have a vegetable and flower garden, and a tiny farm: goats, chickens, pigs, bees."

Shocked, Maura said, "I never would have expected to find a farm at a convent."

"Be open. Be curious."

Maura dressed hangers and filled drawers with the clothes from her suitcase, then slid the suitcase under her bed. She placed envelopes and stationery on the desk alongside some pens.

"You can write all you want, Maura," Eileen said. "But you can't send anything. Remember, we are cloistered."

At seven o'clock, after dinner service, Maura and Eileen Cecilia Brosnan joined other residents for a welcome reception. Young women mingled with old in a large room. Age quite accurately foretold a woman's rank at Regina Mater. The youngest girls, teenagers mostly, were aspirants; postulants were a few years older than that; and novitiates—some having taken their First Vows—were older still. If a woman was thirty years old or older, she had likely taken her Final Vows and was a full-fledged nun, easily identifiable in her dark tunic and habit.

During the reception, aspirants presented sweet faces crowded with wonder and fright; their large, nervous eyes sought companionship. Sister Constance made her way around the room, conversing with all of the new girls, making sure they were getting acquainted and acclimated. Before the reception ended, the nuns broke into song once again, finding music a fantastic medium for speaking to and praising the Lord. Maura knew the psalms and hymns well; she had been singing them in church all her life. A few of the aspirants wept while they sang, though Maura could not be sure if homesickness or the Holy Spirit had caused the tears.

Throughout the evening, Maura reminded herself of Eileen's advice. She imagined herself as an open door and welcomed the evening's events with interest. She missed her family, as well, but recognized that she had gained a new family at the convent. The song called for listeners to lift their hearts to God, to thank Him and praise Him, and to see Him in everyone. Maura made a concerted effort. "You shall never want when you eat the Bread of Life," she sang.

The women, led by Sister Constance, continued singing as they processed in two lines to Corpus Christi Chapel, a marble, stone, and stained-glass structure, topped with the steeple Maura and her family had seen on the drive in. The chapel resembled a miniature medieval cathedral—small, intimate, haunting—with long wooden pews able to accommodate some two hundred people. The chapel's interior glowed from candlelight and a single electric spotlight coming out of the rafters, which illuminated the altar and a life-sized wooden crucifix, the chapel's focal point. The sisters entered the pews and knelt, palms pressed together, heads tipped forward. Aspirants watched and followed suit. Sister Constance guided the congregants through five decades of the Holy Rosary followed by intentions—for the poor, the sick, and the recently deceased. Some of the dead had been sisters at Regina Mater, their full names now read aloud in the chapel—Sister Rita Nadis, Sister Mary Novak, Sister Carol Ann Trufano—and followed by a collective plea: "May God welcome these and all of His children into the light of His face." It struck Maura that these praying nuns had been well acquainted with the deceased, had trained, prayed, dined, and lodged with them, and one day, these same sisters would have their own names read aloud by women with whom they had served at the convent. Maura pondered reading off Eileen's name one day—Sister Eileen Cecilia Brosnan—and praying for her soul. She imagined Eileen reading her name. The thought of death did not scare Maura nor did it sadden her. The old nuns who had stood and spoken the names of dead friends showed no sign of fear or sadness either. Rather, they honored the dead, whose souls had found their eternal reward. Heat bled into Maura's chest and a satisfied smile infused her lips.

The women prayed late into the night. Maura prayed for her family—this one and the one back in Brooklyn. She said prayers of thanksgiving, making no requests of the Lord but simply being thankful and appreciative of all the blessings in her life. When she had done this, Maura felt a tap on her shoulder and found Eileen Cecilia Brosnan beside her. Sister Constance had made no formal conclusion to the evening, choosing instead to allow the women to determine their own end. Whenever a woman finished her own prayers and remembrances, she blessed herself, strode to the altar, bowed, and left the chapel. "Shall I meet you at our room?" Eileen asked. Maura might have stayed longer, but she saw in her new friend's eyes that she wanted companionship.

Neither Maura nor Eileen spoke until they entered the dormitory. Large bronze plaques decorated a pair of pillars leading to the main staircase. Maura had noticed the plaques earlier but now stopped to inspect the names etched there. "What is this?" she asked Eileen. "Who are they?"

Eileen's expression sobered. "They are all of the women who have come here, been trained here, and are buried in our cemetery."

Beside the names were three columns: date of birth, date of ordination, and date of death. Maura studied the dates, finding that these women had given forty, fifty, even sixty or more years of their lives to serving God. One nun—Sister Geraldine Santis—who had died at 103 years old, had been at Sisters of Regina Mater Convent for eighty-five years. The numbers staggered Maura even after she finally got into bed, ending her first day.

∼

Time passed quickly at Sisters of Regina Mater Convent, and yet there were no feelings of being rushed or inundated or overwhelmed. Despite the sisters' adherence to a meticulous schedule, days and nights swayed one into the other, a tepid and fluid movement, peaceful, like changing ocean tides. Prayer and deep spiritual contemplation filled good portions of the women's time. Sister Constance encouraged aspirants to develop their prayerful passion for the Lord, to ask how best to serve Him. As general superior, she understood the importance of bonding for young girls and fostered interpersonal connections and communal activities as ways to increase aspirants' faith and devotion to Regina Mater.

Conversely, nothing upset, saddened, and disappointed Sister Constance more than when a brand-new girl—in a fit of tears and blubbering—said she was not meant for the religious life. Worse still was when a young girl admitted confusion about all things in life, except one: She definitely did not want to become a nun. This did not happen very often, but when a teenager quit the convent, a pall of personal failure followed Sister Constance for weeks, and she sequestered herself in the chapel for long hours of prayer and reflection.

During summer, Maura met regularly with Sister Josephine, the spiritual director, a nun of forty-three years, who shared her thoughts on prayer, devotion, and spirituality. She asked Maura to reconsider the purpose and process of prayer, and continually described prayer as "deep, strong, and powerful," that prayer done well could change one's outlook, could change the world. Sometimes, Sister Josephine would read Bible passages to Maura, and they would analyze and discuss the scriptural meaning and intent, and how those themes might play out in an aspirant's life.

Maura also met with Sister Maryellen, the vocation director. Sister Maryellen, a nun for twenty-one years, joked that she was—in religious terms—practically brand-new herself. The woman had amiable eyes and a compassionate personality, always recognizing and validating others' points of view, even if she disagreed with those views. Sister Maryellen asked Maura to consider her long-term vocational interests, anything from helping Brazil's orphaned children to sharing Christ's teachings with Angolans to serving in a Long Island hospital. In the short-term, Sister Maryellen placed Maura on the farm detail.

Maura felt blessed to be outside for the summer and to be working on the convent's small farm. After morning prayer and breakfast, Maura, along with some sisters, tended the goats, chickens, and pigs. The pigs could not have been happier munching scraps left over from the dining hall. Maura scattered feed and collected chicken eggs in a large woven basket; she also milked the goats and learned how to make cheese. After caring for the animals, Maura worked the large garden, cultivating cucumbers, tomatoes, strawberries, watermelons, string beans, corn, and eggplant. And the work never ended. Once one crop was harvested, another sprouted and ripened, and a good farmer, Maura learned, always planned a season ahead; already the summer soil had to be tilled in preparation for the fall crops: pumpkins, more corn, cabbages, onions, and a host of herbs. One-third of the garden contained colorful and sweet-smelling flowers, too, which, Maura discovered, responded to a gentle, nurturing hand. While she worked the soil, Maura thought about her family, her sister, Kathy, in particular, who hated to be outside in the summer lest she sunburn and freckle. Kathy would, however, appreciate a tulip's tangy aroma or a purple violet's gossamer petals but only from a shaded spot.

The Sisters of Regina Mater also operated a day camp at the convent. Four times per week, buses unloaded scores of children between the ages of six and twelve. The kids embarked on nature walks through the convent's woodlands and learned about varieties of trees and shrubs. They observed caterpillars and inchworms, chased butterflies and chipmunks. They spotted blue jays and cardinals and red-winged blackbirds and shrieked at occasional encounters with garter and ribbon snakes. In addition, the campers ate lunch in the dining hall, completed arts and crafts projects, played ball games and hopscotch, and jumped rope on the blacktop. And invariably, they loved visiting the farm.

At first, Maura was shy, even afraid, when the children came running toward her. Their energy and enthusiasm and gleeful screeching shattered the convent's pastoral mood. She gladly let the other nuns and novitiates answer the children's questions:

"Why do violets have to be purple?"

"What are the goats' and pigs' names?"

"What is the difference between a rooster and a chicken?"

"Why don't the chickens fly away?"

"Are those tiny strawberries real?"

After a few weeks, Maura grew more and more comfortable addressing so many children at once, and when they bombarded her with questions, she admitted when she had no answer. Her honesty seemed to satisfy the children. Perhaps the best thing that Maura did for the children was involve them in farm work. She gave children opportunities to enter the animal pens; they were invited to hold a chicken if they could catch one. Maura had children scattering feed and carrying buckets of goats' milk and collecting eggs and berries and beans, mint and oregano and basil. The children muddied their knees and hands tilling soil and pruning or potting plants, seeding and watering the land. The only thing that Maura wouldn't do was allow herself or the children anywhere near the beehives.

The change in Maura's behavior toward the campers started with two very specific children. The boy and the older and taller girl were not siblings but could have been with the way they clung together, often holding hands, except when signaling to each other with wrist curls, hand flips, and finger jabs. They shared the same rare and beautiful auburn hair and complimentary freckles. The girl reminded Maura of Kathy.

Curiosity compelled Maura to approach the pair, who maintained constant separation from the larger group. "What are your names?"

They ignored Maura.

"What are you talking about?"

The children knelt in the garden, huddled around pale-pink geraniums, mumbling quietly and moving their hands into different shapes. Maura studied them, stepping around to face the children, smiling as she lowered herself into the dirt. She held her pointer finger to one ear and brought it to her lips, signing to the pair, "Are you deaf?"

The children noted the gesture but only stared back somewhat fearfully. Maura signed and signed again, but when the boy and girl still did not comprehend, Maura wrote her name in the soft garden soil, then signed each letter for the pair: M-A-U-R-A.

The kids signed back: S-E-A-N and P-A-T-R-I-C-I-A.

Sean and Patricia had developed a corrupted communication system, partly derived from standard sign language, partly from invented slang signs. They could sign most of the alphabet and many common words and expressions, but their knowledge of standard sign language was incomplete. The kids could understand about half of what Maura signed and vice versa. But, at that moment, the similarity was enough to found a friendship.

～

Dear Kathy,

If you haven't noticed, the days are getting shorter. Dawn and dust grow chilly, and the day-campers have made their last visit to us for the year. In our garden, corn and pumpkins and potatoes flourish.

The honeybees foretell the end of summer by working overtime, racing against some instinctive, internal clock. I have gotten more comfortable with my garden partners and admire their work ethic. The bees—who don't bother me as much—hurriedly pollinate plants, buzzing here and landing there, always competing against waning daylight. As soon as the sun hints at setting, the bees speed back to the hives, their workday done. Cooler temperatures appear to subdue the bees and quiet their temperament, and this late-day lethargy gives me courage to approach the hives.

Sister Eva Howard, who has the most experience working the farm, mentors me. One afternoon a few days ago, Sister Eva and I donned beekeeper suits, complete with mesh veils and helmets. I felt like a Martian in the outfit but followed Sister Eva to what looked like a set of squat, wooden filing cabinets, painted varying shades of green.

"All I want to do," Sister Eva told me, "is show you the honeycombs, and if she'll allow it, we can glimpse the queen." As Sister Eva worked open the first hive, the rather placid bees became more active. They zipped and looped about, buzzing ever louder. But I felt safe in my suit, and whenever bees landed on my gloved hands or long sleeves or mesh veil, I stayed calm. It was weird what happened, but after a while, I crossed a threshold of some kind, as if I had passed inside of a funneling tornado and found a totally peaceful core.

I had my first look at the inside of an active hive, saw the queen bee, and the waxy honeycombs—honeycombs dribbling with honest-to-goodness honey! I was so excited and asked Sister Eva why we don't harvest the honey. She said it was a good idea, but she didn't have time for such an undertaking. Maybe I'll give it a try.

Love you, miss you,
Maura

September was at hand, and Maura and the other aspirants were automatically enrolled in the convent's novitiate college. Known as Regina College, the school consisted of one large academic building with an enrollment topping out at 250 students. All but a few of the students were women from the convent. Sister Constance believed good nuns were educated nuns and pressed for all the women to attain bachelor's degrees. The curricula offered women apostolic training as well as degree tracks in arts and sciences, including nursing, criminal justice, and social work. Nuns, priests, and laity staffed and taught at Regina College, and with a full semester course load, Maura Moloney became very busy. She excelled in English literature, biology, and theology; St. Mary's Academy had prepared Maura well, and even though she struggled to learn Latin, college appealed to her quest for personal growth.

In actuality, Sisters of Regina Mater Convent contained everything Maura craved. She communed with God in frequent prayer and reflection; she made dear friends with women young and old; she grew stronger in the faith she had been practicing all her life; she learned gardening and farming; and in a few years she would receive a college degree. In less than three months at the convent, Maura was absolutely certain that she wanted a religious life.

Once autumn began in earnest, nothing could stop it. Leaves turned orange and yellow and, before long, flung themselves from boughs. Maura celebrated dawn mass, attended college, met Eileen Cecilia Brosnan for lunch, worked the farm in the afternoon, returned to the chapel for evening devotions, and completed homework assignments either in the library or in her room. Despite her packed schedule, Maura continued to write letters to her sister, Kathy. Of course, she could not mail the letters during this time of sequestration, but the act of writing proved to be another kind of meditative, prayerful practice. Putting thoughts on paper soothed Maura, and she knew that when she saw Kathy again, she would refer to this epistolary record of important life moments. She wrote about the plants and animals, about her school lessons, and her new acquaintances. She tried and tried to explain in words the stirrings inside of her—"as if the core of my soul were opening, shifting, expanding, like a fist loosening, like a heart swelling. My soul is receiving His light for the first time"—but felt she could never accurately capture her own development.

Regardless of any writing deficiencies, Maura thrived in her new home.

～

Though a white Christmas had been forecasted, not a single flake fell upon the convent grounds. Maura had been unable to sleep the night before. She had been unable to quiet her anticipation and, after morning mass, entered the library, which afforded an expansive view of the convent's main entrance. For the first time in six months, the gates had been pulled back, and by mid-afternoon, families had begun arriving. Maura watched impatiently from the library perch for her father's black Chevy.

When she could sit still no longer, Maura put on her winter coat, gloves, scarf, and hat and took a stroll, hoping to expend her surging energy. The squirrels, hard at work picking through frosted grass and darting along bare tree limbs, appeared equally energetic and anxious. Maura followed a paved path, one she had come to know well in the last few weeks, and arrived at Regina Mater Cemetery, a rectangle of earth buffered by a fence and surrounding woods. Nuns, reared and trained at the convent, had been laid to rest there, and Maura found comfort in the symmetrical layout: white headstones arranged in long, straight columns and rows on a pale-green field. These women, all of them, had devoted nearly their entire lives to the Lord, and their graves called to mind a history to which Maura suddenly felt connected. These women's souls surely resided in paradise, and Maura exalted that her paradisiacal journey had begun. She peered down at one of the many white, arched headstones imprinted with the word "Sister." Beneath was the departed's name, Mary Louise Barten, and below that a botonnée cross separated the year 1869 from 1950. Sister Mary had been eighty-one years old.

The chilly wind brought tears to Maura's eyes and returned her to the present moment. She strode out of the cemetery, horrified by the thought that her family had arrived and she had not been there to greet them.

~

Despite the bare boughs and yellow lawns, Kathy thought the convent looked palatial in the diminishing afternoon light. Her father had to park the Chevy a good distance from the main building since all of the closer spots were taken.

Kathy, her parents, and her little brothers—who were wearing tiny brown suits and buffed penny loafers—entered the lobby and met Eileen Cecilia Brosnan and her family straightaway. Eileen took coats and handed back coat-check tickets. Kathy asked if Eileen had seen Maura. She could not stand to be apart from her older sister any longer. Eileen said, "If Maura's not in the library or on the farm, she's out for a walk."

Kathy considered turning in her ticket, taking back her coat, and searching the grounds for Maura, but as she turned, she found Maura ascending the lobby steps toward her and her family. Maura embraced her parents first, then her spiffy brothers. Kathy charged toward Maura, who stopped her. "And who is this?" Maura asked and signed.

Kathy could not tell if she was being serious and sarcastic.

For the occasion, Kathy had curled her hair in such a way that thick strands looped past her collarbones. She wore a brand-new dress that she (with her mother's guidance) had stitched from scratch.

"You're taller," Maura said.

"Almost as tall as you now," Kathy bragged.

"And your face. What happened to your chubby baby face?"

They laughed.

Kathy took hold of Maura's arms and looked her over. In her own way, Maura had become a grown woman. It wasn't envy that stung Kathy then but anticipation. She saw her own development in Maura's development, her future in her sister's present.

Prior to the Christmas feast, relatives and guests joined the Sisters of Regina Mater in Corpus Christi Chapel for the Christmas Eve Vigil Mass. Monsignor D'Zazzi, who had been saying mass in the diocese for almost forty-six years, led services. Monsignor D'Zazzi progressed through the mass with all of the aplomb, grace, and dignity befitting a clergyman. He moved about the altar slowly, aware that he was just a guest in the house of the Lord, that he was a servant not the master, and he took seriously his actions, genuflecting and bowing and making the sign of the cross with all due humility and sincerity. Further, Monsignor D'Zazzi shunned lavish, pompous, and excessive ceremony. Instead of a blaring organ and grand musical score, he asked the choir to sing just a few songs a cappella, and instead of belaboring the vigil, he intentionally and expeditiously moved through the course of the mass. Even his homily had been pithy, reminding congregants of John's Gospel: "He who believes in me, even if he dies, will not die." At that moment, Kathy peeked at Maura and found her sweeping a tear from her eye. As the vigil concluded, Monsignor D'Zazzi stood at the chapel exit, so he could shine his beaming eyes and crooked smile on the faithful, and personally greet each one of them. The silver-haired monsignor stayed for the Christmas feast, but only briefly; he wanted to rest before saying Midnight Mass at St. Bartholomew's Church.

Kathy and her family ate and talked almost unceasingly. Her parents gave updates about the neighborhood and about relatives. Her brothers told Maura that they were enjoying elementary school and looked forward to the next morning when they could tear into their Christmas gifts. Kathy had much to tell Maura but wanted to hear Maura's stories first. What was convent life really like?

Although she struggled to learn Latin, Maura otherwise adored studying, especially the English poets Coleridge, Keats, and the Brownings: Robert and Elizabeth. She talked extensively about her work on the convent's farm and in the garden and gestured to the buffet. "The potatoes, the winter squash, the onions, half the food on your plates came from our little farm," she said. "Isn't that amazing? And just recently, I have become something of an apiarist. My hope is to begin bottling honey in the spring."

Her brothers called out: "Take us to the farm, Maura, won't you?"

"Sure. I'll even let you feed the goats."

More than anything, Kathy wanted to talk with Maura in private, the way they had done while sharing a room back home. She asked Maura to give her a quick tour of her room. The girls went off together, and after admiring Maura's living quarters, they parked on a wooden bench at the end of a quiet hallway.

"A lot has changed," Kathy began. "You won't believe it, but all of a sudden, I love school. If I knew what being a senior was like, I would have skipped all the other grades. Seniors are admired, respected. Classes are easier. The teachers know I am your sister, and since we look alike, they assume I am as smart as you are. In general, I'd say senior year at St. Mary's feels like a year-long victory lap." Kathy went quiet, studying the cuffs of her sweater. Without looking up, she signed to Maura: "Do you remember Robert Marginella: tall, shy, a lopsided smile? His father owns a pizza shop."

"He's sweet on you, is that it? Are you madly in love with Robert Marginella?"

Kathy raised her face to Maura.

"I am just teasing, Kathy. I only want happiness for you."

Kathy inhaled slowly. "I broke up with Robert after Thanksgiving."

"Broke up?" Maura lifted her left hand, fingers splayed, and with her right hand ticked off each digit, the sign for "details."

Robert Marginella's mother had told Kathy and Maura's mother that Robert thought Kathy was cute and wanted to take her on a date. The mothers talked to the fathers, and once all the parents agreed, word got back to the teens. Robert had come to the house wearing a dress shirt and suit coat, his dark hair still moist from having been run-through with a wet comb. He had given Kathy a gift box that contained a plush teddy bear. The pair had walked five or six blocks and dined on mushroom-and-pepperoni slices at Marginella's Pizza. Robert had paid the tab with money borrowed from his father.

"We went on some dates," Kathy said and signed, "and Robert was nice and all, but . . ." Again, Kathy studied her sweater sleeve, picking at the stitching. She changed the subject. "Are you really going to become a nun?" Kathy didn't know why, but for some reason, she was skeptical about Maura's decision.

Surprise lifted Maura's eyebrows. "How can I explain," Maura began. "What can I say that will help you understand how I am feeling?" She brushed a hand over her lips. "I'll just say it: I *love* this place! This is where I belong, and every day at Regina Mater confirms my choice. The enjoyment I feel each morning and the thankfulness each evening are almost overwhelming. I am blessed." Maura snatched Kathy's hand. "I am blessed to be a member of this community. Did you know that a group of us spent last Friday in the basement of St. Bartholomew's Church, serving meals to the homeless? I am energized by our community's devotion to prayer and contemplation. The women here, their tender hearts and generosity, impassion me. The farm and garden are my sanctuary. I am going to earn a college degree, and in a few years will officially become a nun and make a tangible difference in the world. Really, I could not be happier! This was the best decision of my life; it has changed my life." Maura was gasping, crushing Kathy's hand.

Silence followed.

"Do you want to know why I ended it with Robert Marginella?" Kathy asked, speaking deliberately. "There was no connection. I couldn't love him because I wasn't attracted to him. I got to know Robert and let him know me, but I wasn't drawn. Do you see? I wasn't called." Kathy felt her cheeks burn. "Do you remember," Kathy went on, taking her hand back and rubbing away the pain, "when we were here last, when we dropped you off here? Do you remember when I met Sister Constance, and she asked me about joining the convent? Do you remember? Well, I do. I have been thinking about Sister Constance for six months. Maura, my life has changed, too, since last we talked. Home is not the same; school is not the same; I am not the same. I thought I wanted to date Robert, but once I did . . . I thought I wanted to go off to college, but once I began filling out applications . . . I have been thinking a lot lately about my future and my choices, and maybe that life"—she jerked a thumb over one shoulder—"back in Brooklyn is no longer for me. Maybe *this* is the life for me . . . just as it is for you. Maybe we *are* twins, you know?"

With fingers splayed and palms up, Maura signed and said, "What are you saying?"

"I am saying that I am thinking of becoming a nun . . . like you . . . joining the convent."

The sisters hugged, and restrained, high-pitched squeals—a harmony of shock and delight—passed between them.

"Do Mom and Dad know?"

"No. I haven't told anyone but you."

"This is incredible."

"I know. But don't say anything to anyone. I'm not totally ready to . . ."

Maura advised Kathy to pray and read scripture, to speak with any of the sisters at Regina Mater or the ones who taught at St. Mary's Academy; even Father Brennan or Deacon Lombardo at their Brooklyn church could help.

"I know. I know," Kathy said, trepidation creeping up her spine.

"Well, you'll figure out what works best for you."

"Maybe we should head back to the dining hall; it's getting late."

They rose from the bench together and walked back to the celebration, their heels echoing in the empty corridor.

"Now that I love high school," Kathy said with a chuckle, "what if I became Sister Kathy Moloney, teacher at St. Mary's Academy? That would be outrageous."

The girls reached the dining hall just as Sister Constance finished an announcement at the podium. ". . . and that is why I have furloughed all of the aspirants, postulants, and novitiates until the Feast of the Epiphany, what I call 'Women's Christmas.'"

A rousing applause echoed through the hall, and that night, when Kathy and her brothers got into the back seat of the Chevy, Maura was beside them.

Once in Brooklyn, Kathy and Maura were inseparable. They spent considerable time walking the neighborhood, reuniting with friends and former classmates, and romping through the New Year's Day snowfall. Their mother made lavish dinners and invited over friends and relatives, as if Maura were royalty. Maura freely engaged people about her first six months at Sisters of Regina Mater Convent, how she loved praying and reading, studying and farming, socializing and serving. She discussed her passion for the religious life with anyone willing to listen.

Kathy stayed mute about her interest in a religious life and regretted even mentioning anything to Maura. She preferred instead to behave as she always had, like a typical teenager. Kathy quickly grew tired of listening to her older sister profess love and longing for the convent. At one point, Maura even proclaimed that she favored Regina Mater to Brooklyn. Whether she meant the comment or not, Maura seemed more like a proselytizer than a sister, always trying to persuade and cajole. If Kathy ever joined the convent, she would do so of her own volition.

~

Maura and the Sisters of Regina Mater prayed seven different times on the Feast of the Epiphany and spent three hours in the chapel celebrating Women's Christmas, which, Maura learned, is known in Ireland as Nollaig na mBan. Sister Constance intentionally de-emphasized the Roman patriarchal Three Kings Day tradition in favor of a more Gaelic and maternal ritual, where women lit candles and chanted ancient phrases for ecclesiastical prosperity, spiritual guidance, and communal well-being. And they prayed fervently, clapping and singing and swaying, until the candles burned low. Afterward, the women dined on black pudding and thick slices of currant bread smothered with blackberry jam, washed down with cups of tea.

The entire feast day had Maura thinking about her sister back home. Prayer revealed to Maura a plain truth: She undoubtedly wanted Kathy to join the convent. The admission put a smile on her face that frequently reappeared. Maura already loved the convent, and to have Kathy accompany her on the journey . . . the possibility felt so indulgent that a groundswell of guilt chased away most of her good feelings. How could she ask the Lord for so much when so many in the world had nothing? Rather than pray for herself, she should pray for the vulnerable and the enslaved. Maura hated to think she was being selfish, and over the next several days—with prayer and contemplation—Maura trained herself to table her needs, to silence her racing thoughts, and—as spiritual director Sister Josephine advised—Maura dedicated herself to studying, silence, manual labor, and the community of sisters. If she was not listening to a lecture, Maura was completing homework assignments. She nurtured the farm animals and honeybees and awaited the first thaw in order to till and sow the land for spring harvest.

The weeks passed quickly, and by the time Maura looked up, the lion of March had become a lamb. Days grew longer and warmer. At Regina College, professors began talking about final projects, papers, and examinations. The chickens on the farm produced more eggs and the bees produced enough honey to bottle. And Maura's prayer muscles enlarged. She had developed the ability to delve into prayer with speed and economy. No longer did external concerns distract her; no longer did she struggle to block out the noise of the world, but like one entranced by the snap of a finger, Maura needed only to close her eyes to find the light of His face.

As the semester concluded, Maura shifted more of her time to the farm and garden. She had succeeded in filling a dozen eight-ounce jars with pure, raw honey. The goats produced enough milk to make goat cheese, and the flower garden yielded bouquets of petunias, impatiens, geraniums, and begonias. Maura had gone to the general superior with the idea to open a farm stand to the community. "Only, I think we should 'give' rather than 'sell,' Sister Constance."

Sister Constance hastened a response: "Very well, Maura."

Despite all of her hard work farming and readying a produce stand, despite struggling through a forty-five-minute oral and written Latin examination, despite a month-long, concentrated, prayer devotional in the Virgin Mary's honor, despite time spent with Eileen Cecilia Brosnan cleaning the chapel or dormitory, and despite contemplative strolls out to the cemetery, Maura still had fleeting thoughts about her sister, Kathy. Still cloistered, Maura and the other aspirants were forbidden from contacting family. She could write all the letters she wanted but still could not send them.

Dear Kathy,

I cannot stop myself from wondering if you are still interested in joining the convent. Or, has the interest faded? Has the idea of becoming a nun passed away like some of your other career ideas have?

You should be getting ready to graduate from St. Mary's Academy and contemplating where next your life might lead. Whatever you are thinking, I am dying to know! I reach out with my thoughts, hoping to connect with you telepathically, like twins are said to do, but no definitive responses ever come back. I guess, Kathy, you either still want to become a nun or you do not. God bless.

Hugs and kisses,
Maura

∾

June was hot, and suddenly so. In another month, Kathy would turn eighteen, and much sooner than that, she would be graduated from St. Mary's Academy. Each Sunday since the spring, Kathy had spent more and more time praying after mass. She had been asking God for direction, for a sign, and had been keeping ready a keen ear and vigilant eye to receive the message.

Kathy waited for her father and little brothers to leave. For months, her father had been promising his sons a trip to Flatbush to see the rubble that had been Ebbets Field. They would be gone all day. Kathy met her mother at the wall-mounted telephone and signed, "I need to place a call. Will you help?" Kathy never used the telephone since her deafness made telephones pointless, that is, unless she had a translator.

"Did you say 'call'? Who are you going to call?"

Kathy dialed. She and her mother stood side by side, the handset pressed between them. When the line engaged, her mother signed the greeting.

"Yes . . . hello . . ." Kathy couldn't steady her quivering voice. "This, ah, is Kathy Moloney. Hi, Eileen. Do you remember me? I am Maura Moloney's sister."

Eileen remembered, then apologized. "I am sorry, Kathy. I cannot connect you with Maura. We are cloistered, you understand.

"No, I wasn't calling for Maura. I was calling for me, to report that I have decided to join the convent."

A stream of tears steaked her mother's face, and she placed a hand over her nose and mouth to keep from crying out. On the other end of the line, Eileen congratulated Kathy, said she would add her name to the list of attendees. "Maura will be so happy."

When the call ended, her mother hugged and kissed Kathy with ferocious enthusiasm. The jubilant daughter and mother danced themselves breathless. "I am going to make a feast," her mother said. "Oh, but first I have to call everybody and spread the wonderful news. No one is going to believe this!"

~

A customer at the farm stand placed some dollar bills in an empty pint-sized berry basket.

"No, thank you," Maura said to the woman with gapped incisors and sturdy eyeglasses. "The berries are free; the flowers are free; everything is free. Please, keep your money."

The woman refused to rescind her offering, saying, "Lord knows I could be more charitable." She walked away while snacking on blueberries.

Other patrons also made donations, paying whatever they could. Maura didn't know it yet, but from that day on, she would always find berry baskets brimming with dollar bills. The good fortune was wholly unexpected yet much appreciated.

Eileen Cecilia Brosnan reported Kathy's decision to Maura, who found Kathy's commitment to the convent also unexpected and appreciated. However, when it came to Kathy's arrival, Maura found that waiting was the hardest part. Try as she might, she could not stifle her impatience. During the days following Kathy's phone call, Maura flitted about, smiling and staying busy, but at bedtime, Maura failed to calm her thoughts and consequently could not sleep. She became so impatient, so frustrated by the infinitely long days, that she called on spiritual director Sister Josephine for guidance, who said the only thing she could say: "Pray deeper, stronger, more powerful prayers." Maura, next, called on Eileen Cecilia Brosnan for prayer support. "If we combine our prayers," she told Eileen, "maybe we can accelerate time," but when that did not work, Maura prostrated herself and beseeched the Father Almighty for the strength to endure.

∽

Just four days before the new aspirants would arrive for their welcome luncheon, Kathy—again with her mother's help—called the convent a second time, greeted Eileen Cecilia Brosnan, and kindly asked to speak to Sister Constance. Kathy's mother had agreed to sign the phone call on the condition that Kathy would lead the conversation. "You are an adult now, Kathy. You are responsible for your actions."

The general superior answered, and Kathy's mother signed the greeting to her daughter.

"Sister Constance," Kathy said, "I made a miscalculation. I got the dates wrong, and, well, I have a previous engagement that I cannot break. I won't be able to attend the welcome luncheon."

"Previous engagement," Sister Constance said, and Kathy's mother signed the words.

"Yes, Sister Constance. I have plans."

"'Plans,' you say?"

Kathy's mother—arms bent at the elbows, hands extended as if for a double handshake—made a right-to-left sweeping motion, the sign for "plan."

"Young lady, what plans are more important than God's plan?"

"I am to attend a wedding on the same day as the welcome luncheon."

"A wedding?"

"I'm sorry. I am completely at fault, Sister. I have known about the wedding for months and should have told you sooner but—"

"Are you lying?"

"No, Sister." Kathy could not believe the accusation.

"Some girls lie to themselves, but God knows the truth. Do you realize how important the welcome luncheon is? Missing your first day means you can miss the second day and every day after. It means you can quit before you start. We at Regina Mater do not take our commitments lightly. Do you have a passion for the Lord, Kathy, for serving Him?"

"I do, Sister." Kathy felt her voice crack; she began to sob. "I promise I do."

After a pause, the general superior's tone softened. "Maybe it would be best to send a gift to the engaged couple in your stead. I am sure they would understand your absence."

Kathy's mother batted the dangling middle finger of her left hand with the pointer finger of her right hand, the sign for "absent."

"Yes, Sister Constance, but I am *in* the wedding party. I'm the maid of honor."

A second, extended pause followed, then the general superior said, "Just ask the bride to postpone the wedding."

Kathy panicked. One would have to be mad to make such a preposterous demand on a woman less than four days before her wedding. Simply, it would be quite impossible to change the wedding ceremony now. The hall was rented, the church reserved, the hotel rooms booked, the band retained, the honeymoon paid in advance. No, it was not possible. The bride-to-be might just perpetrate some heinous assault if Kathy even broached the subject.

Sister Constance relented. "Very well, young lady. Go to the wedding. But by five o'clock on Sunday I want to see you in my office. No excuses."

Kathy thanked Sister Constance repeatedly and, after the call, dabbed her cheeks with a tissue from her mother. But as Kathy left the kitchen, she could not decide what caused the tears: gratitude and relief or reluctance and dread.

⁓

The day of the aspirants' welcome luncheon arrived, and Maura was awake early. She attended morning mass in Corpus Christi Chapel, ate breakfast, and walked out to the farm to collect the flowers that would serve as centerpieces during the welcome luncheon. She spent a considerable amount of time preparing the dining hall and placing the floral arrangements on every table. Yet, while she worked, Maura could not shake the sorrow that slumped her shoulders, sorrow rooted in longing. Shortly, the aspirants would begin arriving with their families and the hall would grow clamorous with conversation. Maura would meet girls from all boroughs of the city, girls full of nervousness, excitement, and wonder, and she would see herself in some of the aspirants and befriend them. But none of them would be Kathy, and no matter how often she glanced at the entrance, Kathy would not appear. Maura would have to wait another day and a half to see her sister, an insufferably long time.

As the luncheon progressed, as people dined and talked, Maura illogically kept looking for her absent sister. Sister Constance introduced Maura to a pair of aspirants from Staten Island, who looked overcome by the entire affair. "It's a little intimidating," the girls admitted, "the convent, the grounds, the buildings, the nuns. We almost broke our commitment."

Maura admitted that just a year ago she had been similarly emotional and offered the same advice Eileen Cecilia Brosnan had given her: "Be open, be curious, and be honest with yourself. If you think this is not the life for you, then it is not the life for you. You can't partially become a nun."

Once more, Maura thought about Kathy and looked toward the entrance, only to be disappointed again.

The luncheon followed the same agenda as last year. Sister Constance spoke, every nun found a new girl to mentor, and a choir of singers carrying candles regaled guests with spiritual hymns. Finally, the event concluded, and parents and relatives made their way out. Maura, along with some other women, volunteered to clean and clear tables in the dining hall; she would have accepted any form of labor as long as it occupied her mind and passed the time. During evening prayers in the chapel—the new aspirants' first experience collectively communing with God—Maura wept, thinking that Kathy should have been present and participating.

After chapel service, Maura planned to take a flashlight and tour the farm one last time that night, but she unexpectedly felt exhausted and returned to her room, where she fell into an uneasy sleep.

Morning came and with it the realization that Kathy should be arriving that afternoon. Maura pulled her wristwatch from the nightstand but could not believe the time. She had slept through morning mass and breakfast and had not yet visited the farm. For the entire year, she had never neglected her duties and obligations. She had always been punctual and prepared, dedicated and committed. "Oh, God," Maura said repeatedly, flying out of bed, dressing, and dashing out the door and across the grounds.

Some of the other women had taken care of the farm stand, opening early and stocking the baskets and barrels with eggs and lettuce, strawberries and carrots. Maura apologized for her tardiness and immediately jumped into position. The other women, including Sister Eva Howard, declined the apology, saying, "Maura, we knew you would show up. You have never let us down before."

But I did today, Maura thought to herself.

By three o'clock, a man in tattered, untied shoes accepted the last of the produce and shuffled away. Maura began tidying the stand, preparing to close for the day, when Eileen Cecilia Brosnan came hurrying toward her, gasping, tearing, sniffling, saying, "I'm sorry, Maura . . . I'm sorry. I just got off the phone . . . with your mother . . . I couldn't find you." She pushed a fold of paper into Maura's palm. "Oh, I'm sorry."

Maura brought the note close and delicately unfolded it.

"I am . . . praying for you," Eileen said. "I have been praying the whole way out here."

Just three words written in pencil filled the scrap of paper. Each bubbly, looping, cheerful letter of each word belied the dreadful message: "Kathy is wavering."

Tears blurred Maura's sight, scrambling the horrible message. A single, fat teardrop landed on the note, and Maura refolded the paper, sealing sadness inside. She staggered away from the farm stand toward the dormitory, parsing the universe of meaning in those three words.

∾

Nearly twenty-four hours earlier, Kathy stood upon the altar at Holy Souls Catholic Church in Brooklyn. She was joined by Father Sutter, the bride and groom, the best man, and two altar boys. The boys, in white albs with gold cinctures, held brass-finished processional candlesticks topped with budding flames. Though more than one hundred and fifty finely dressed people filled the pews, Kathy ignored them. The ceremony—the opening procession and musical accompaniment; the stately, regal atmosphere; and the resplendent, white wedding gown—had captured Kathy's attention, put her in a state of heightened focus. With deep intensity, she read Father Sutter's lips as he spoke of love: God's love for mankind, the filial love that brought bride and groom into the world, and the romantic love that joined them today. Kathy fantasized that she was the bride, that this was her wedding.

Before continuing the ceremony, Father Sutter asked for the people on the altar to huddle together, shoulder to shoulder. "This circle is our unbroken bond," he said, then, to the wedding couple, added, "Let's begin with consent, shall we?"

The bride and groom—pale with nervousness—nodded. Kathy nodded, too.

Father Sutter said, "Elizabeth Margaret Ahern and Nicholas Ryan Pappas, have you come here to enter into the marriage sacrament without coercion, freely, and wholeheartedly?"

"We have."

"Are you prepared, as you follow the marriage path, to love, honor, and obey each other for as long as you both shall live?"

"We do."

"Are you prepared to accept children lovingly from God and to bring them up according to the Law of Christ and His Church?"

"We are."

At the same time, Kathy had been making her own internal declarations: I have, I do, I am.

"Since it is your intention to enter into the covenant of Holy Matrimony, join your right hands, and declare your consent before God and His Church."

Elizabeth handed off her bouquet to Kathy and gave her hand to Nicholas. Kathy tightly gripped the bloom of white roses and edged a bit closer.

Father Sutter opened his palm, and the best man placed a pair of gold rings there. The bands overlapped, forming a Venn diagram that made the priest smile. "Elizabeth," Father Sutter announced, "do you take Nicholas for your lawful husband, to have and to hold, from this day forward, for better, for worse, for richer, for poorer, in sickness and in health, until death do you part?"

The heft of the moment slowed the bride's reply; Elizabeth appeared to study and savor each phrase and each circumstance, letting the meanings pour through her.

"I do," Kathy whispered, certain God was calling her to a life outside of the convent.

The bride and groom turned their eyes to Kathy, so did the priest and best man. Even the altar boys looked away from the mesmeric candle flames. Disbelief and embarrassment seared Kathy from the inside. They had heard her; she had spoken aloud! A long second of intense unpleasantness passed. Kathy fumbled for mercy. "Oh, um, sorry," she said abashedly.

Father Sutter slanted his eyes back to the bride. Elizabeth, with emphatic tenacity, said, "I do," as if overruling the previous utterance.

The ceremony continued.

Kathy withdrew into herself, berated herself for her own foolishness. She believed that she did not have the passion that Sister Constance required, that she had come to this wedding not just to avoid her decision but to end it altogether. Anything but total commitment to the sisters, she knew, was a sacrilege. She could not partially become a nun.

In the reception hall rest room Kathy prayed and cried and asked God why life included such tremendous doubt and pain.

The next day, Kathy took ill and could not get out of bed. Her mother phoned Regina Mater and asked Eileen Cecilia Brosnan to relay a dire message to Maura.

~

Kathy is wavering. The message rang in Maura's head, and she half wished she were deaf, so she wouldn't have to hear the merciless taunt. She bypassed the dormitory in favor of the chapel. She would speak to Christ, pray for compassion, plead for the anger and hurt within to simmer and cool, but when she reached the doorway, she found the interior brightly lit and the choir at practice. Maura carried herself to the empty library. Wavering meant that doubt had subverted conviction and disbelief had distorted faith.

With tears dripping from the corners of her eyes, Maura entered the library and found her usual panoramic perch. Outside the window, shadows stretched across the grounds of the convent, the orange sun dimming every minute, squirrels skittering here and there. Five o'clock had come and gone. Maura sat with her feelings, allowed herself to cry. She recalled the girl—Bridget—who had been crying on the front steps last year when Maura and Kathy and their family got out of the Chevy. After just one day, Bridget had quit the convent. Who could say what had brought Bridget to Regina Mater and so quickly dispatched her? She must have been terrified, hopeless, lost. She must have been wavering, too. Where was Bridget now? Maura wondered.

Maura slumped against the wall, her cheek to the window, tears streaking the glass.

Movement sparked at the edge of her vision. Another tear, she thought, plumping and waiting to spill out of her eye. Maura peered across the grounds, caught a flash of reflected sunlight in the ornamental grill of a black car that had just come through the entrance gate. With her thumbs, Maura swept away tears and, looking again, saw her father's Chevy winding its way toward the parking lot. The car veered into a spot and stopped, and Maura stopped, too, paralyzed with disbelief, watching from the window high overhead. Could it be? Could it be?

～

Her father opened his door and stepped out, put on his suit coat and gray hat. She watched her mother and brothers get out of the Chevy, too, before she pulled the door handle and emerged herself. Kathy, in a white blouse and long, plaid skirt, brought a single suitcase into the main building's lobby. She looked up in time to catch a person—Maura!—hurtling toward her. The sisters embraced until Kathy protested. "I can't breathe. You're breaking my neck and wrinkling my outfit."

"What are you doing here? I received a message—"

"I prayed and listened and felt God's presence. I had an epiphany; there's no other way to say it."

Their father said, "We would have been here sooner, but the traffic—"

"I prayed, too!" Maura said.

"I was unsure before," Kathy said.

"And now . . . ?"

"I am sure." Kathy emphatically pushed a vertical finger away from her chin, signing, "*Very* sure."

The meeting with Sister Constance started poorly for Kathy. Sister Constance castigated her and launched into a lecture about passion and commitment to the faith. The typically controlled general superior unleashed disappointment and displeasure, saying several times that she believed Kathy was unfit for the religious life. Kathy had no rebuttal, could offer no counterargument, and when it looked like Kathy would have to return home with her parents and brothers, Sister Constance said, "When I look at you, Kathy, I see your sister, and that gives me hope." She permitted Kathy to stay. Later, Kathy told Maura that she had needed the scolding, that the whole episode had ultimately shocked her, spurred her maturation, and granted her clarity. From then on, Kathy conducted herself decorously.

～

However, the process of becoming a nun had not been effortless. Originally, Kathy—advised by vocation director Sister Maryellen—planned for a nursing career. She pursued and earned a degree in nursing from Regina College in four years but was not assigned to any of the local Catholic hospitals. She met with Sister Constance to learn why.

"Let me start," Sister Constance said, "by saying that I wanted you to become a nurse just as much as you do, Kathy. But"—she gestured to the phone on her desk—"then I got a call from the bishop, and I must admit that he has a point. Imagine this, Kathy: You are a nurse, a fine nurse, in the maternity ward at St. Vincent's, for example, and you do your best to monitor the newborns, to keep them safe, but you can't watch them all the time, and one of the babies, one born prematurely and undersized, is struggling, fighting to live, crying at the top of its lungs, wailing for attention, for nourishment, for love. Maybe this poor child is dying and needs you—the nurse on duty—but you don't come because you are deaf and can't hear the calls for help." Sister Constance waited a long time before speaking again. "Deaf nurses do not exist. A nurse needs all of her faculties. You understand, don't you?"

"But I can read lips, and I won't take my eyes off of those babies and . . ."

Kathy was devastated, and had Maura not been there to comfort her, to pray for and with her, Kathy might have had a completely different life. Well, in actuality, she did have a completely different life.

Initially, Sister Constance harangued the bishop, pleaded with him for an exception to his ruling on deaf nurses, bragged about Kathy's abilities, but when that failed, she turned, through prayer, to God, and a new idea appeared instantly. Sister Constance called a follow-up meeting with Kathy.

"I have just received permission from the bishop to open a new school at Regina Mater, a school for deaf children. Would you be interested in leading the effort?"

Kathy said nothing.

"We are calling the school St. Catherine of Alexandria School for the Deaf. She is a patron saint of teachers and students and was a skilled debater. You won't become a nurse, Kathy, but you can become a teacher."

Though originally discouraged, Kathy saw potential in the appointment and, after a day, accepted the post. St. Catherine of Alexandria School for the Deaf began with two students already familiar to the

Sisters of Regina Mater, having been day-campers the years prior. Patricia, now twelve, and Sean, eleven, became the very first students, and Kathy their teacher. Two more children joined a month later, and by the start of the second year, twenty-five deaf children had enrolled. Naturally, Maura, well-versed in sign language, became a teacher, too, and worked alongside Kathy every day. The sisters considered the school a blessing, a miracle, and committed themselves to its development. St. Catherine of Alexandria School for the Deaf exceeded expectations and so rapidly expanded that a dedicated schoolhouse was built on-site. In five years, the school developed an exceptional regional reputation, and Kathy and Maura praised God for His beneficence.

∼

Maura held the railing as she descended the stone steps of the main building. She pulled her coat closed at the collar, fastened the button there, and dug her hands deep into her pockets. Maura walked the grounds, evaluating the white winter clouds, wondering when the snow would begin, watching squirrels shiver in the bare boughs. She entered Regina Mater Cemetery and stood before a familiar headstone, the word "Sister" arcing across the curved top, a Celtic cross chiseled between the years 1942 and 2006. The name on the headstone still felt like a mistake, but no matter how Maura squinted or blinked or adjusted her glasses, the words remained: Sister Kathy Amelia Moloney.

Kathy had joined the convent in 1960 at the age of eighteen. She had studied there and started a school for deaf children, where she worked and taught for twenty-two years alongside Maura. Because of Kathy's success, in 1986 the diocese appointed her director of Mary's Place, a halfway house for homeless, abused, and formerly incarcerated young women and their babies. For the next nineteen years, Sister Kathy nurtured and supported these mothers and children. She offered shelter and food, companionship, and childcare, as well as referrals to adult education, job training, counseling, and rehabilitation services. She shared, too, her story with the young moms, explaining how she had once been unsure—wavering, in fact—but had sought God through prayer and there found solace and strength in His presence.

Sister Kathy came back to Sisters of Regina Mater Convent, back to Maura, in 2005, after the surgery to remove a cancerous breast. She had been dedicated to her chemotherapy treatments even though they left her terribly sick and frail and bald. Regardless, the second breast was excised shortly after and new cancers materialized in Kathy's liver, kidneys, and stomach. Maura stayed with Kathy to the end when painkillers were the only drugs left to take.

"You were my best friend," Kathy said to Maura, sliding in and out of lucidity. "Did you know that?" Kathy let out a woozy chuckle before pain swelled her face and mangled her features. "We were—" but she could say no more. Instead, Kathy stacked one finger-pistol upon the other, the sign for "sisters."